Puzzles
The Will

A Murder Mystery

Tom Walton

BookLocker

Trenton, Georgia

Published by BookLocker.com, Inc., Trenton, Georgia, U.S.A.

The characters and events in this book are fictitious. Any similarity to real persons, living or dead, is coincidental and not intended by the author.

Printed on acid-free paper.

BookLocker.com, Inc.
2023

"You are all a piece of the puzzle,

in someone else's life."

- Bonnie Arbor

Dedication

To Sonya and Angie,
I miss your laughs and smiles.

Other books by Tom Walton

What Do I Put on My Notecard!
(With Lori Norin)

Defining Moments: Secrets That Should Never Be Told

Defining Moments II: More Secrets That Should Never Be Told

Swedish Gem

Cats: Why We Love Them So

Prologue

Ethel stood on the far left of the stage sharing it with nine other Mrs. Oklahoma contestants. It was getting harder for her to maintain both her dazzling smile and T stance at age 42 than it was when she was 22, but she managed with great effort. Now she had a chance to finally make it to Atlantic City, a Mrs. instead of a Miss. Wearing a red dress with a slit up the side revealing leg and a neckline revealing cleavage, she felt confident of winning.

"Smile and stand tall," she thought to herself. "You're going to win this thing."

She competed in local pageants throughout her college years in the 1950s, winning twice in five tries. She never, however, made it into the top ten at the Miss America pageant. Competing as Mrs. North Tulsa 1975, where she and her husband Herb lived, she won this one more trip to the New Jersey shore of glittery hotel/casinos.

"Oh, I'm so surprised and thankful," she said when interviewed by the emcee as the previous year winner put the crown on her head with bobby pins and placed the sash over her shoulder.

"Finally," she thought to herself as she walked and waved to the crowd. "Make a good turn."

In addition to the paid weeklong trip to the Jersey shore and $2000 cash, she received a pair of diamond earrings worth $1000 each. She managed a top five finish in the Mrs. America pageant and Herb bought her a diamond ring to go with her earrings as a concession prize.

"You are the love of my life," he told her as he gave her the gift. "You are beautiful and I'm proud to be your husband."

1

Herb was promoted in 1977 to detective after 10 years of being a beat cop. He had earned the promotion for being the leading police officer in a drug bust that kept over three million dollars of cocaine, heroin, and opioid pills off the streets of South Tulsa.

"Just being at the right place at the right time," he said during the press conference. "It was a real team effort and I thank all the officers who participated."

Ethel served as a counselor at a local university until she had to retire in 1992 at age 62 due to a severe stroke. After a year of intensive rehab in which she had to relearn how to walk, write, and eat, the doctors suggested that it might be best for her if the two of them moved to a retirement community.

"There are plenty of independent living facilities in this area," said her doctor. "With an aide coming in once or twice a week I highly recommend it for you."

Since Herb still had about 15 years of working ahead of him, he was 10 years younger than Ethel, they decided it would be a good option to move instead of trying to maintain the large family home of over 2400 square feet with a big yard that Herb maintained himself.

Their two children Audry and Andy were both adults now with their own families, and they agreed wholeheartedly it was time due to circumstances for Herb and Ethel to sell the house and move.

"Do it," said Andy. "Don't think about it, just do it."

Audry echoed her younger brother's sentiment. "Go, go, go."

Herb had grown bald. He kept trim and weighed between 170 and 180 pounds every year at his physical. His son, age 28, was already showing signs of going bald and had ballooned to over 240 pounds. Both were just under 6 feet tall.

Audry, on the other hand, had inherited her mother's charm and good looks. She had long, black wavy hair just like Ethel, and long legs, too. At 32, she still looked like she was in her early 20s.

Ethel and Herb, along with Andy and his wife Jackie and Audry with her husband Matt, spent the next month touring all the independent living facilities in the Tulsa area. They agreed on the Piedmont Tower as the best option. It was a 15-story limestone building built in the 1980s. Off to the side of the building, it had plenty of garden space and a stocked pond. This thrilled both Ethel and Herb because they loved to grow their own vegetables and he fished.

While they visited a flock of geese honked and landed in the pond much to the delight of all of them. Bill, the manager walked around with the six of them. He was fascinated to hear that Ethel was a former beauty queen and that Herb was a police detective.

"Let's go inside," said Andy. "I want them to see everything again."

They passed the shuffleboard courts, the picnic areas complete with built-in grills, the horseshoes area, and the gazebos on the way back in.

Once inside, they headed for the large rec. room for coffee and donuts. It had a complete kitchen and enough room to set up tables for 200 people. There was a big screen TV and piano at the far end. Four ladies played a dice game at one of the round tables and three men played cards at another.

After a brief respite the tour continued. Under the west wing on the ground floor there was a library, computer lab, and laundry room. The library contained books, magazines, movie DVDS, music CDs, and jigsaw puzzles. The lab had 20 computers and four printers. The laundry room featured six coin-operated washers and dryers along with a two vending machines, one for candy and chips and the other for cans of soda.

The east wing held two smaller rec. rooms, a kitchen with lounge for staff, the mail room, a beauty shop, and a small grocery area stocked with toiletries and various OTC products.

There were also three offices on the ground floor between the two wings for the manager, assistant manager, and security guards. A counter space ran along the outside of the offices with windows along the whole track. The adjacent lobby had couches, chairs, and tables on one side with restrooms. There was a big mirror between the restroom doors. There were four elevators on the other side with a fake fireplace in the corner. It could put out cold air during the summer and hot air during the winter.

Ethel and Herb would live on the top floor of the west wing in an end apartment. Farthest from the elevators and lounge which sat between the two wings it was close to the stairs, a small laundry room, and vending machines.

Ethel was 62 and Herb 52 in 1992 when they moved into the tower. He walked a swift two miles every weekday morning before going to work, eight laps on the walking trail around the tower. Ethel, hampered by her stroke, could only make one lap on her rollator. She would go back to their apartment and put on her oxygen and take her pain pills while Herb finished. There was another walking trail that went around the garden, pond, and picnic area.

For the next 16 years Ethel actively participated in playing cards, shuffleboard, horseshoes, and bingo in the evenings when Herb was home. She baked cookies, mostly oatmeal raisin, and along with her best friend Agatha, who also lived in the tower, passed them around in goodie bags to all the residents each Christmas and Easter. She spent as much time day or night visiting in the office and with residents as they came and went in the lobby as she spent time in the apartment.

In 2008 Ethel, now 78, got very sick and Herb, 68, retired to take care of her. A year later, though, he died suddenly. He and Ethel had just finished playing Yahtzee and Scrabble. She went into the kitchen to make coffee. Herb shouted her name and said "Oh no, no." Ethel heard a thud and when she went back into the living room, she saw Herb laying on the floor. She called 911 for an ambulance and then the security guard downstairs to have Herb's paperwork ready for the EMTs. By the time they arrived, Herb's lips had turned blue, and he had stopped breathing. Since he had a DNR in his paperwork, the EMTs could do nothing. One of them asked Ethel, anyway, if they should try to bring him back.

She said "no," and started to cry. "He's gone."

His death really took a lot out of Ethel, and she quickly regressed to a wheelchair. She spent more and more time in the apartment. Her weekday smiling walk around the tower trail with her head held high turned into only forlornly buzzing slowly about in her wheelchair once a week from the front door past the first row of the parking lot to the closest sitting area only about 50 yards from the entrance.

Her yakking to anyone she met along the way about this and that had also regressed to her only looking down and occasionally offering an empty, "Hello, I'm doing as well as expected" to anyone who tried to engage her in conversation. Not even egging her on with a discussion about politics or religion could get her riled.

Over the next ten years, she gained over 80 pounds from not being active and eating out of boredom. Her feet, ankles, and legs swelled due to an extreme case of edema, and she needed the use of oxygen more and more. She also increased the number of pain pills she took each day.

Her graying still wavy hair had turned white and stringy from not being kept up. A musty housecoat replaced her smart-looking outfits. She always, however, carried a can of diet soda in the holder of her wheelchair, and smoked cigarillos.

She had stopped wearing her diamond jewelry that a necklace had been added to by Herb on Y2K night to celebrate the upcoming last year of the historic and frightening for many millennia. She asked Herb how he could afford such an expensive gift, but he brushed off the question.

"Don't you worry about that," and then he repeated what he had said years before. "You are the love of my life. You are beautiful and I'm proud to be your husband."

2

A loud explosion shook the west wing of the tower and frightened all the residents at home that Tuesday morning in mid-August of 2015. It even startled the few who were working in the garden or walking around the pond. The geese shading themselves beneath a tree near the pond flew and the feral cats who were getting a drink of water from the pond scurried into the nearest culvert for safety. From the lobby, the sound seemed to come from the top floor. All the management on duty rushed up the elevators from their offices and ran down the hall of the top floor. Sure enough, it was Ethel's apartment.

"She must have lit a match to smoke one of her cigarillos," said Mike, the manager, to Norma, the assistant manager, as he opened Ethel's door. "And the spark caused an explosion."

"She might have used an alcohol-based hand sanitizer and then fiddled with her oxygen equipment," surmised someone in the crowd that was forming.

Someone else muttered, "It might have been something else."

There wasn't much left after the explosion which contained itself to just her dwelling. The windows were blown out in the bedroom where she was found, and everything was destroyed. The fire department and police authorities, who arrived at various times during the rest of the day, carefully inspected the charred debris. It proved futile. They discussed their lack of findings and reported to Mike and Norma that it was an accident with "cause unknown" because they couldn't find any viable clues.

The adjacent apartment to the left received no damage, much to the surprise of everyone, especially the maintenance staff and contracted workers who would have to repair it. The outside walls to the back and right since it was an end apartment faired just as undamaged except for the bedroom windows.

Ethel's daughter and son-in-law, Audry, and Matt, were known for being "all bark and no bite." They fussed about all sorts of things over the years. The couple, only two days after the accident, threatened legal action against everybody and anybody associated with the tower. They stormed into Mike's office three days in a row, hurling unfounded accusations left and right. He felt obligated since he was new to the position to hear them out.

"Maybe this will help them blow off steam," Mike thought to himself as he prepared to try and be an empathetic listener.

Audry and Matt soon settled down and after talking with both Mike and the authorities admitted Ethel's death was just a horrible accident. When they received the insurance policy death benefit, they were heard from no more. Ethel's son Andy, and his wife Jackie, agreed to go through the apartment one more time to see if anything was salvageable before it was redone for new residents. They found nothing.

3

Mike didn't leave home until his 22nd birthday which came only three days after he graduated from college in 2015. Why should he. If he lived at home and attended school full time, he collected one half the amount of his retired father's social security check. A benefit too good to pass up, and a benefit of being born to parents, Harry, and Evelyn, in their mid-40s then who happened to be in their early 60s when he graduated high school.

Living on the 800 block of Lincoln Street in midtown, Mike attended grade school on the 1200 block, high school on the 1600 block, and would go to college on the 2000 block. He knew he would leave home after college because, as he often joked, "the state mental hospital grounds sit beginning on the 2400 block."

The house at 804 Lincoln Street, like all the others in that neighborhood, had wood siding on the outside painted white with an inside of two bedrooms, one bath, a kitchen, and living room, cramped into 800 square feet. Basements in different degrees of finishing throughout the neighborhood made the houses all seem larger, but they were not.

The elementary school Mike attended, as had his mom and two brothers before him, hadn't changed much since it opened in 1925. In fact, two of the nuns on the faculty that opened the school taught there for over 50 years, spookily dressed in black garb yet smelling like lilac soap, Sister Mary Ignatius, and Sister Mary Herman.

The high school, likewise, sat stoically as it had for over 100 years, but with additions both up and back from the three-story original building constructed with limestone. It was the oldest and biggest of the Catholic high schools in the city. Still not as big enrollment-wise as the smallest of the public high schools scattered around the area.

Mike's mom and two brothers graduated from that high school but didn't choose to go up the street to the university. Mike was the family's first college graduate.

While in college Mike majored in journalism and worked at various small-town newspapers and radio stations all around the area. His social security check, partial journalism scholarship, and minimum wage jobs paid tuition. Plus, he garnered a bit of money from his work/study jobs on the college newspaper, yearbook, tv and radio stations.

Harry, his dad, worked as a salesman at a downtown department store and Evelyn, his mom, as a part-time receptionist in a doctor's office. Neither occupation lent itself to the kind of money it would take to send Mike to college. His two brothers

Rob, and Fred, opted for joining the Air Force straight out of high school. Rob was 20 years older than Mike and Fred was 10 years older. Some people thought Rob was Mike's dad and that his parents were his grandparents.

Mike had two strikes against him while growing up. First, since he was a late-in-life baby he often had to go with his parents when they visited other couples to play cards or have cookouts. Other couples, who had adult children and nobody still living at home. He was banished to another room to sit quietly and entertain himself as the adults did their thing until usually late in the evening.

Secondly, Mike was a preemie, born at seven and a half months, and had health problems throughout his youth that prevented him from playing football, the sport his older and oldest brother flourished in. He did play baseball and basketball but was behind other boys his same age.

With the prospects of college graduation and a birthday coming about it also meant moving out as his parents had been reminding him to do for several months.

"You finally have to look for a real job and a place to live," his dad enjoyed saying a little too much. Both came conveniently, coincidentally, and concurrently.

One advantage he did have as a late-in-life child was that two of his parents' long-time best friends were a retired real estate couple who lived in the high-rise retirement community which sat in North Tulsa. They had negotiated the original purchase of the tower and had moved in upon their retirement last year.

The Harmon's were good friends of the Piedmont Tower owners and board members and felt they could have a say in the process of hiring a new manager. The previous manager had reached retirement age and the assistant manager didn't want the job. The Harmon's strongly recommended Mike for the open position.

"He will knock your socks off," said Art Harmon. "He's very bright and hard working."

"You'll like him a lot," Peggy Harmon added. "We have known him since he was born."

The owners and board members agreed to interview Mike. He prepared for the interview by attending workshops given by the university. He wore a navy-blue suit with a darkish red tie, got a fresh haircut, was clean shaven with no visible tattoo, and had a one-page resume. He was ready with answers of how his classwork related directly to managing a retirement community. He also researched each member of the interview committee so he could make references to their jobs and other community energies when and if appropriate. He had grown into a striking six feet two-inch man which didn't hurt his chances, either.

"Have a firm handshake, an articulate voice void of slang, arrive five minutes early, and be nice to the person at the front desk," were the last pieces of advice offered him at the last session of his preparation workshops. He wowed at the interview and a done deal quickly ensued, much to the satisfaction of all five board members and the two owners who interviewed him.

Mike gladly accepted the position of property manager. He moved into the onsite updated, cleaned, painted, recarpeted, and sprayed-for-bugs apartment. That process took about five weeks, the same time as his training and indoctrination. The former property manager Bill, as Mike was told in no uncertain terms by the owners, had become too lenient and friendly with the residents.

"You as new blood should lay down the law more," one of the owners, a lady named Gertrude of considerable assertiveness, said.

"Have a real come-to-Jesus-meeting right away with both the staff and the residents," added the not nearly as intimidating Charlie, the other owner.

They, and board members, felt a true affinity for the tower and its residents and staff, but stayed away from the day-to-day doings of it and its people.

"You are young, not nearly in the same age range of the residents as Bill was," Gertrude said. "Use that to an advantage."

As directed, Mike first had a meeting with all the staff as he started his job. He asked for them to "openly and honestly volunteer any and all concerns and ideas." They did. It took all his first Monday morning.

He then scheduled an open forum for residents to voice their concerns and ideas. They did, too. It took all his first Friday afternoon.

He asked Norma, the assistant manager, to attend the meeting for moral support and to deal with any issues he wasn't aware of yet. She did but let Mike handle everything.

In between that first week of meetings two residents died, three residents fell, a security guard quit, seven new applicants got put on the waiting list, one of the geese bit a granddaughter of one of the residents, and a case of bed bugs closed off the lobbies of the second and 11th floors.

Norma, the assistant manager, declared she wished to stay in that position since she had her eye on a paralegal job in the suburbs near the airport close to where she now lived. Pregnant with her third child, and not yet 25 years old, she needed more money and the closeness of home that a new job might bring.

Besides, she never really had bonded with any of the residents. She had gone on enough in her life that she didn't get intrigued with listening to the constant stories that the residents harped on every time they came into the office to discuss what she considered minor issues.

When she went to lunch on Fridays with Alma, one of the housekeepers, she would complain about hearing, "oh, it's too hot," in the summertime and, "oh, it's too cold" in the wintertime over and over and that it just didn't fare well with her after three years on the job. That as she also said to Alma, "petty residents reporting petty spats," got on her nerves.

Frustrated after a particularly long day of trying to deal with the aftermath of an early morning thunderstorm that left the east wing kitchen on the ground floor flooded by torrential rains and 70 mph winds, she had to hear every resident who came in the office tell their story about experiencing winds, floods, or rains.

She complained to her husband that night when she finally got to go home, "whenever something happens at that place, I must listen to countless accounts of how it happened worse to them somewhere and sometime else."

She and her husband Larry, who worked at the nearby zoo as a feeder in the big cat area, had married right after high school graduation with her three months pregnant. They had recently bought their first house after living in Larry's parents' basement for nearly seven years.

Her decision left the property manager's job and an onsite apartment empty. Since a member of management had to live onsite, it fit perfectly into what Mike needed.

Norma had been head cheerleader in high school and Larry, a three-year starter at defensive end for the football team. He latched onto her midway through junior year and their hormones got the best of them. They tried to only "get together," as they described it to their parents, the first three days every month after Norma had her period, but it didn't work once, and she got pregnant. Larry Jr. was born during Thanksgiving week of 2010. Next came Norman in July of 2012, and now Joey whether boy or girl would arrive in early December.

The owners and board members of the tower had agreed they wanted to inject some new ideas into the management anyway. They had no intention of offering the job to Norma, but they didn't let it on to her that they could tell she was not happy being there. They thought an eager, fresh-out-of-school newcomer would be a good idea instead of someone who would be, as they all felt in discussing the job description, "the same old same old."

4

Bill, the property manager of Piedmont Tower, who held the position since 2002, announced his retirement to begin at the end of the fiscal year in June. He and his wife Gladys often in those last days on the job talked about moving out of their onsite two-bedroom apartment. They had plans, as they told most everyone, to move to Florida to live, ironically, in a retirement village on the Gulf of Mexico side of the state.

"We'll celebrate our 45th wedding anniversary in our new digs," said Gladys at the retirement luncheon organized for them by the owners. "It's been quite a journey since the old days in New York."

"I'll say," said Bill. "I may even let my hair grow out a bit."

The luncheon catered by a local BBQ restaurant attracted most of the residents and filled the big recreation hall on the ground floor that had been set up with tables and chairs.

"I don't know if you came to say goodbye or because of the free food," Bill joked. "Anyway, we look forward to our move south. But we will miss you all."

He had held a manager's job for over 25 years before that at an aging hotel in lower Manhattan. He met Gladys there. She would walk by the front of the hotel every morning at about 10:45 to go to the dance studio next door. Bill got infatuated by seeing her always wearing orange or purple dance socks over her tights. He got up the nerve one day to go out front and talk to her. It went well and she invited him to "come over anytime to watch the practice sessions."

He did and less than a year later of a whirlwind courtship in the "Big Apple" they married. After the tragic events of 9/11, the twin towers only a few blocks from the hotel, they moved to North Tulsa thinking it would be far from any danger.

Except for his widow's peak crew cut turning from brown to gray, his 144 pounds soaking wet only going up to 149 pounds, and his right leg limp slowing him down a step, he remained the same. Nobody knew the reason for his leg, but rumor had it that something happened in Vietnam during his younger years in the military, a time of his life that he reluctantly referred to but didn't elaborate on.

Gladys, standing even smaller than Bill, barely reached 5 feet tall and weighed just under 100 pounds. She had short black hair and reminded folks of Judy Garland. Not only for her looks and size, but because she could sing and dance. An athletic woman she taught dancing classes part-time at the university.

She had the run of the tower and often would be seen in the library, computer lab, hairdresser's, kitchen, and the lounges of each floor. She talked to any residents she saw. She seldom got on the elevators, though, preferring to run up and down the stairs instead.

"Got to keep in shape," she would say jokingly. "I don't want to have to use a cane or rollator any time soon."

"Your day will come," Bill said.

5

Malcolm, the new security guard chief who usually worked the graveyard shift during the week, spent some of his time on duty at the office talking to the residents who couldn't or didn't sleep much at night. They came down to the lobby at various times in the early mornings mostly to hear him talk with his accent and to see what food he brought with him to snack on during his mostly quiet eight-hour shift. Malcolm, claiming to be pure Scottish, reveled in flaunting it.

He said he grew up in Dunfermline, a city of 60,000 in Fife, on high ground three miles from the northern shore of the Firth of Forth. He had the red hair and light complexion of the Crawford family that traced back to the 17th century, he would say. He was short and skinny, only 5 feet 6 and about 150 pounds.

He explained that when his grandfather began tracing the family tree and found out that his grandfather served as the parish rum runner, he had a penchant for saying to his grandchildren, "If the apple doesn't fall far from the tree." It was at this point that Malcolm said he came to America to go to school. He chose Oklahoma over Kansas or Arkansas.

In his best brogue he would repeat an old Scottish saying, "a day to come seems longer than a year that's gone."

Malcolm wanted to study criminology but after three semesters of taking mostly gen. ed. courses with tuition, books, and fees mounting up, he decided to quit college and find a job. He landed the security guard gig in less than a month.

Thanks to Mike and his directive from the owners to inject new, young blood into the management and staff, Malcolm was quickly moved up to chief to replace the stodgy, old man who had held the job for over 20 years. He had grown a bit too staid and serious-minded to fit in with the fresh new wave of leadership.

Malcolm often brought Scottish Pie a double crusted mincemeat pie made of mutton. He also would bring Cullen Skink consisting of smoked haddock cooked in heavy cream with potatoes and onions. But Haggis was his favorite.

"I've heard of it but don't know what it is," said Agnes when she stopped to talk with Malcolm on her way back up to her room after being outside walking laps.

"All I know is it's nasty," said Amelia, Agnes' smoking friend.

"Boiled sheep innards with root vegetables sort of like potatoes and turnips," Malcolm told Agatha and Amelia. "They are called *neeps* and *tatties*."

The ladies who 'burned the midnight oil,' would rather listen to his stories than sample his culinary concoctions, but they enjoyed the camaraderie. Of course, he was as prone to bring candy bars and other candies to work, too. That would lead to heated discussions on rather milk chocolate should be on most candy bars instead of dark chocolate, white chocolate was just as good as milk chocolate, or whether dark chocolate should be the preferred kind.

He walked four laps around the tower every morning after his shift to "work off my cravings for chocolate bars."

The 'night owl' ladies would invariably bring samples of their favorite foods made from traditional family recipes. The lobby smelled like a buffet many late nights and early mornings. Debates would carry on about the merits of rye bread vs. Texas Toast when serving barbecued ribs, be they pork or beef, whether fried tenderloin sandwiches should be made from beef or pork, and the inevitable question of whether peanut butter cups were better than coconut cups or crème-filled cups.

But the longest and the most frequent stories centered on the 'things that go bump in the night' that he heard some of the residents experienced. He would tell, with great flair, about the strange noises reportedly heard in the stairwells, the noises purportedly heard in the laundry rooms emanating from behind the vending machines, to footsteps coming from the roof or behind walls of apartments.

6

One night while Lulu and her neighbor Rae were sitting in his office, Malcolm told a story about a man who used to live on their floor.

"One of the security guards even had to investigate the complaint that old Morris heard the humming of the theme song from *Sesame Street* coming from behind his bathroom," Malcolm related.

"Old Morris only a month earlier stormed toward my desk from the lobby elevator claiming he awakened at 2 a.m. to someone whistling while scaling the outside of the building knocking on windows," Malcolm continued.

"It turned out to be birds chirping at a woodpecker," Malcolm laughed.

"Are you kidding me?" Lulu almost shouted. She then started laughing almost hysterically. "Maybe we should call Billy Bud."

Billy Bud was the bed bug inspector. A frequent visitor to the tower because of random infestations, he gets called three or four times a year to check and, hopefully, find out the number of apartments with evidence of bed bugs. A problem that kept, "creeping and crawling up," he joked.

He was on site so many times a year that he seemed like part of the management team.

"I'm sort of like the copy machine repairman in an office suite," he said. "Onsite so often that I might as well be in the staff picture."

It took him almost two weeks to make the rounds on each floor checking for bed bugs in every apartment. The tower had 15 stories excluding the 13th floor. There were 16 one-bedroom apartments per floor with two two-bedroom apartments, one on each end of the wings. There were no apartments on the ground floor. 208 singles and 26 doubles to inspect.

He was known as "Billy Bug" by most of the residents who had been living in the tower long enough to have been around for his previous visits. He also had been given another nickname in the last year – "Kleptomaniac Man."

New residents particularly reported small items missing after he had been in their apartment. Nothing major usually just ashtrays, salt and pepper shakers, and packaged snacks that happened to be sitting out on the kitchen cabinets. Sometimes it might be a bar of soap from the bathroom, a roll of toilet tissue, or an empty pill bottle. An occasional pen, cigarette lighter, or candle would disappear.

He was a short, skinny man like Malcolm. He had light brown hair, but with a streak of gray evident on the right side of his short beard. He said that Memphis, a small west Texas town on Highway 287 near Childress was where he was from. He wore a raggedy Texas Tech hat, overalls with lots of pockets, and a Dallas Cowboys jersey underneath.

He had a long fingernail on the pinkie of his right hand, but insisted when asked that it was just for looks.

"Not what you think, nope," he would say shaking his head vigorously.

He always did a thorough job inspecting. First, he would check all the furniture in the living room, even turning over chairs, loveseats, and sofas to check the bottoms with his "magic light," as he called it. Next, he would go into the bedroom and tear down the bed slinging the sheets, comforters, and pillowcases every which way after looking at them. The mattress and box springs, if there was one, was next. They would get put back sort of in place after he looked at them, but not the sheets and all.

He had a good sense of humor and loved to talk with anyone who would banter with him. Sometimes there would be someone in the apartment when he arrived, and sometimes not.

7

The Harmon's had quite a history before they came to North Tulsa in the late 1970s to start a real estate company. Originally from West Chester, a suburb of Philadelphia, they attended Catholic schools together from Kindergarten through La Salle University where they majored in finance. Art grew up playing baseball, basketball, and football through high school. Similarly, Peggy grew up playing softball, basketball, and volleyball, also through high school.

They married during their senior year a week after being crowned homecoming queen and king. They both worked in one of the dining halls on campus throughout their university studies. After graduation they bred bulldogs and worked as landscapers for a home builder for five years.

Just like the university nickname, the Explorers, Art, and Peggy decided to leave Philadelphia and head west with no idea where they would end up.

"Let's just drive ten hours today and ten hours tomorrow," Peggy suggested as they crossed the Potomac River on the first leg of their journey.

"Sounds like a plan," agreed Art.

"We'll start our own business wherever we are then," she added.

The first day they drove I-81 south and turned on I-40 west with a layover near Knoxville, Tennessee.

They decided to settle in North Tulsa, the closest big city to where their trek ended in eastern Oklahoma between Sallisaw and Vian, and they started a real estate business. Specializing in commercial property, they got in on the ground floor of a new mall, two apartment complexes, and a retirement community. Duplexes and housing developments soon followed. They owned their own agency building within ten years. By the time they retired in 2014 they had over 50 agents and were one of the biggest selling companies in the city.

They had arrived at the right place at the right time and had a successful life for themselves. Time now for them to enjoy their retirement years and four grandchildren while they both had good health.

Art and Peggy only had one daughter, Shirley, who was married to the local symphony orchestra conductor. They had four boys who all opted for playing musical instruments instead of playing sports. A cornet, violin, trumpet, and bass fiddle occupied the boys' time. Each one aspired to play under the wand of their dad, the maestro.

8

Lulu was bipolar. When she had a manic period, she was hard to take. Full of energy and going nights without sleeping she would spend almost all that time downstairs talking with Malcolm. Something he didn't enjoy much because most of what she said was "ugly talk," as Rae, her next-door neighbor and buddy on the 8th floor who came down with her called it.

Lulu ended up in the tower when her son and daughter could no longer handle her episodes. When in a manic mode, she would call one of them in the middle of the night and either talk about having visions and hallucinations or ask them to take her to a casino. When in a depressed mode, she either wouldn't answer the door or phone, or would go without eating. Finally, after almost a year on the waiting list, her name came up for an apartment at the Piedmont Tower.

Lulu had just divorced her third husband and was living alone in the tower. Her son and daughter arranged for her to have an aide. Her name was Madge and she specialized in dealing with manic disorder patients. Lulu kept Madge reasonably in check, but sometimes "had her hands full," as she would say.

Lulu during one of her episodes at the tower called her aide every name imaginable. She had not let Madge in her apartment when she came to check on her. She locked the door, put a chair against it, and refused to open it claiming she didn't know any Madge and that she was probably a terrorist.

Madge was the most patient person ever with 20 years of experience dealing with those who suffered from manic behavior. She talked very calmly and non-threateningly in the hall to Lulu.

"Hey, Lulu, this is Madge and I'm here to finish checking on you just like I did yesterday," she said.

"I don't know who you are," hollered back Lulu from inside her apartment. "You go away, or I'll call the police."

Madge called Paul, the security guard on duty. He came right up. Rae had heard the yelling and came from next door. She offered to help if she could.

Madge continued to talk with Lulu trying to remind her of familiar things that would, hopefully, spark cooperation. Lulu continued to escalate the threats against Madge.

Madge told Paul that Lulu was probably suffering from a TIA and would get over it in less than 30 minutes.

"Talk in a calm voice," she reminded Paul.

"Lulu, this is Paul, the security guard. If you'll please open your door a crack, you can see your aide Madge and your neighbor Rae."

Paul looked at Rae and nodded his head to her. This served as a cue for her to intercede.

"Hi, Lulu, this is Rae," she said in the sweetest voice she could muster. "It's almost time for us to play cards."

"Remember," Rae continued, "You won one of the games yesterday."

"Why did you call security?" Lulu screamed. "I have a baseball bat."

Paul repeated his message for the next 10 minutes, but Lulu didn't relent.

Madge and Rae quietly stood vigil outside her door, but Lulu still threatened them. "I know you're out there. Go away and leave me alone. You'll never get to me before I get you."

Paul whispered to Madge, "Does she have a gun?"

Madge whispered back, "No, she doesn't. She is all bluff when she's like this."

"She'll be fine in a little while," said Rae.

Paul reluctantly left the scene, Rae went back into her apartment, and Madge went down the hall to see her next patient.

Sure enough, in about an hour Lulu opened her door and went downstairs to check on her mail. She smiled and talked to Paul as if nothing had happened. She saw Rae, who was coming in from a walk, and they talked like the buddies they were.

On the extreme when Lulu was in her depressed state, she never spoke above a whisper, slept all week, wore the same pajamas for the whole time, and spent nights just sitting in the lobby not talking to Malcolm or droning quietly from time to time.

During Mike's open forum Rae, a non-smoker, suggested making the entire tower and its property smoke free. Only the top floor housed smokers and they could also gather any place outdoors so long as they didn't throw their cigarette butts or matches on the grounds. This policy came about when the tower first opened because the original owner Max was a heavy smoker and sensitive to the needs of fellow smokers. But his son Max Jr. a non-smoker, and one of the owners now was leading the trend to "clean house of the old ways."

Rae went to the same church as Max Jr. and knew his wife Claudette from childhood when they lived in the same neighborhood. Because she knew Max Jr., she felt entitled to be a bit bossy. She didn't have many friends of the residents who had lived at the tower for years. She made it a point to get to know all the new residents as they moved in and offered to have them join her contingent of church goers. Most were thankful for her fellowship and did, and some were offended by her self-righteousness and didn't.

Lulu, a smoker, during one of her lucid periods, suggested that a designated smoking area be made available just off the property boundary. Both ideas received loud approval, and most of the smokers agreed. But not Ethel. This occurred over a month before the explosion. She rambled on complaining with a fervor she had not mustered in years.

"I don't want to have to go out in the heat, cold, rain, or snow to smoke my cigarillos," she said. "What goes on in the privacy of my apartment is my business."

Lulu called Ethel "an old bitty" and Rae had to intercede to keep a badmouthing duel from starting.

"Now, now ladies, let's not be this way," she said. "Let's keep cool heads."

All it would take to create a smoking area Mike found out from Lopez, the head of the maintenance crew, would be taking out a section of the metal fence that defined the property and putting up a gate in its place.

"No problem senor Mike," said Lopez. "I will call the shop tomorrow to find out a price and how long it will take to make one."

A safe location with trees on one side and an open area on the other side easily accessible from the walking paths got chosen.

After the meeting Rae talked to Mike and thanked him for being so assertive in adding what she felt were important and necessary new policies.

"I'm so proud of you," she said.

9

Mike felt a little excited about implementing a new policy that would impact everyone. He decided on doing them as they came up two a month on the first and 15th. He would write about them in the monthly newsletter and announce them on the intercom.

The first ones starting in August would be the smoking policy and the pet area policy. Next to the east wing of the building would be a gated dog park area complete with all the accouterments with residents responsible for picking up and disposing of their pet's "business."

The policy read that, "dogs must be leashed and small enough to be transported in a buggy from the apartment to the park. They must be supervised by their owner or aide while in the park area."

On the west side of the building a cat park of equal size and with an equivalent array of equipment would be fenced. The same rules would apply to the cats. In addition, cats would no longer be allowed to wander around the hallways of each floor on Sunday evenings from 7 p.m. to 8 p.m. with the doors to 'their' apartments left open.

The policy went on to say that pet deposits would increase from $150 to $200 a month to cover the new costs incurred, and residents may have only one pet per apartment. Pet deposits, however, would be waived for those who presented a need-for-an emotional-support-pet letter from their doctor.

"Dogs and cats must be spayed or neutered, and owners must show proof of their pets' shots and yearly checkups," the policy also said.

It concluded with, "Anyone having something other than a dog or cat must get additional approval from the property manager."

Mike discovered that a lizard, mink, bunny, ferret, and talking parrot also resided in their midst.

"At least nobody has a snake," he said to Norma after he found out about the other animals. "Now I know why the housekeepers say it's like a zoo around here."

Mike decided the pet policy would be announced first and the smoking policy second based on pet owners outnumbering smokers 44 to 31. It ended up being a fatal error.

August 1 the pet policy went into effect with only mild displeasure from a few. Dogs got used to being put in a buggy and strolled out to the dog park. They needed a leash at first to stay in the buggy, but quickly got used to sitting relatively still until they jumped free in the fenced-in dog park. Only a few tenants had dogs bigger than the buggy and they lobbied successfully to be allowed to quickly walk them leashed so the pets didn't stop along the way to do their business.

Cats had to be transported to their fenced in area in a carrier and then set free to roam around. The 12-foot fence kept them away from the clutter of feral cats that wandered about and lived underground with access through the culverts in the parking lot. At first the resident's cats didn't want to go back in the carrier, but eventually they figured out the routine that they got to go back to 'their' apartment. Catnip in the carriers helped, too.

Mike thought incorporating parts of the existing policies with new ones would soften the blow for both pet owners and smokers. The smoking policy took effect August 15 too late, it seemed, to save Ethel.

Pearl, who lived just below Ethel was one of the ladies that took her death hard and was terrified by the explosion above her.

10

Pearl thought the ghost of her dead husband Bert visited several times a week. He died in 2007 after a two-year battle with leukemia, but she claimed for the next eight years that he came by sometimes in the afternoons but usually late at night.

"I hear him, don't tell me I don't," she insisted.

When she first asked Mike to come up to her apartment on the 14th floor to "hear the noise for yourself," he declined.

"He's getting older, and I worry about him," she said. "I hear him in the bathroom."

"Are you sure it wasn't just Ethel upstairs using her bathroom," explained Mike. "Or it could be the wind whirling around the corners of the building," he added. "I sometimes hear noises, too."

"Ethel's dead," she screamed. "She blew herself up. I thought my ceiling was going to cave in."

"I know, Pearl, but I'm talking about before," Mike said in a calming voice. "It might even be someone on the stairs."

"You don't believe me either," she snapped. "You're just like Bill."

She continued to hound Mike. He finally relented one late Tuesday afternoon to go with her up to her apartment. He had to pass by apartments with dogs barking at the sound of his footsteps outside their doors or TVs blaring because most of the elderly were hard of hearing. This floor, like his on the second floor, had doors covered with wreaths or cute cat signs like, "Dogs have masters, Cats have staff."

As he approached her apartment, he noticed the sign on the door to the stairs missing. He opened the door and looked inside to see if it had fallen there. He didn't see it but noticed dirty shoe prints instead. He made a mental note to have Lopez clean them up and replace the sign.

Pearl's apartment smelled musty and looked dusty. An odor of rotten food came from the kitchen. There were several empty pill bottles on the counter next to the refrigerator. Another smell of dirty clothes came from the bathroom. Mike could hardly stand it. The Scentsy burning of cinnamon didn't cover the odors. There were more empty pill bottles in there, too. Covers on the sofa and chairs had stains and rips. Nothing he saw matched what she looked like or how she carried herself. He worried that her apartment might be a candidate for one of the bed bug infestations. He made a mental note to alert Billy Bud the next time he came to inspect.

Pearl walked with her head high and had a swift, confident pace. You could tell she visited the tower's hairdresser regularly. She wore gold and diamond rings on both hands and always had on a pearl necklace. Her stylish pantsuits made her look trim and 20 years younger than her 83 years.

She had been a salesclerk at a jewelry store for over 25 years in a city in Arkansas. The store originally was on the main drag downtown, but moved to the new mall in the early 1970s on what was becoming the next main drag in the center of town.

She and Bert moved to North Tulsa in 2000 to be closer to their kids who had settled only 30 miles to the east along Highway 169. They hooked up right away with Ethel and Herb. He even served as one of the pallbearers when he died.

Mike quickly looked in both the bathroom and bedrooms where Pearl said she heard Bert. He knocked on the walls, looked at the ceiling, and even called his name much to the delight of Pearl who watched him closely with her piercing eyes.

He finally admitted to her that he didn't see or hear any signs but that he would have Lopez look around when he came by to put another "In case of fire use the stairs" sign on the stairway door and clean the shoe prints.

After Mike left, Pearl cooked some leftover spaghetti sauce she had placed in the freezer, boiled some macaroni, and toasted a slice of garlic bread. She ate supper while carrying on a conversation with Bert, as she had done many times before.

"I wonder what is on the TV tonight?" she asked. "I hope we can stay awake."

After cleaning the dishes, she settled on the couch and turned on the TV to watch a rerun of MASH, Bert's favorite show. Before it ended, she fell asleep.

Delores, who moved in at the beginning of the year on the 12th floor below Pearl's apartment, couldn't sleep because Pearl's TV was still blaring at midnight when she went to bed. Delores had been on the waiting list for nine months. She also needed two bedrooms, like all the apartments on the end of each wing because her grandchildren sometimes spent the night. Also, she had two out-of-town daughters that occasionally came for week-long visits.

Unlike Pearl, Delores looked 20 years older than her age of 61. She had a bun of graying hair, about as broad as she was tall, and wore house coats all the time. She moved slowly but always had a smile and cheerful "Hello, it's nice to see you" greeting for anyone she saw.

Her in-town daughter Rose, a nurse who worked all shifts and needed a babysitter for her two little girls, looked younger than her 27 years. With long, brunette hair and suntanned skin she caught the eye of many of the elderly men. None of them of the age or deportment to stand tall and suck in their guts.

11

Rose had two daughters, identical 8-year-old twins named Trudy and Lucy. They both had jet black hair just like their daddy. They all had lived near downtown in an older house that had been converted into a duplex ever since Rose's divorce the year before.

The house had a big, fenced backyard safe for the girls. They frolicked a lot playing with the dog that lived next door and the two cats that occupied the other side of the duplex.

The next-door neighbors allowed the girls to go in their backyard to get their dog JoJo when he went out. Half beagle and half dachshund, he had a double name and a bark that spoke volumes. By his looks and slow movements, one could tell he had never missed a meal.

"He really needs the exercise time because he barely fits any more through his doggie door," said Purnia, the lady who lived next door with her husband Zebo.

The cats who lived on the other side of the duplex were neutered tuxedo brothers. They stayed indoors during the day and went from window to window to follow the girls when they ran around in the yard. At 4 o'clock when Tanya, the college girl who lived there came home, she let the cats out and they either played with the girls or went exploring based on their whims and moods of that day.

When Delores moved into the tower the girls, used to a big backyard and the freedom to be rambunctious, roamed the hallways, elevators, and stairs. They wanted to walk all the dogs and cats and didn't hesitate to knock on any door that housed one.

Loud but cute they spent more time running around all the floors saying "Hi" to everyone they saw than napping or playing quietly in their grandma's apartment. Sometimes they drew pictures and colored quietly in the stairwell, not being seen nor heard for hours at a time.

The residents of the 12th floor as well as anyone in the lobby or outside the front entrance could tell what shift Rose worked by the loud arrival of her and the girls. If the voices and running footsteps began about 7:30 in the morning, waking up some and not disturbing others depending on the hearing levels of those in bed, then Rose had to work the day shift from 8 a.m. to 4 p.m. If all seemed quiet during the day and the voices and footsteps could be heard late in the afternoon, then Rose had to work the evening shift from 4 p.m. to midnight. Occasionally the little footsteps and giggling could be heard along with Rose screeching, "hush, girls be quiet" if she had to work the graveyard shift from midnight to 8 a.m. Lights out was 11 p.m. and the hallways and lounges were supposed to be dark and quiet. Either way, coming or going, giggles and running could be heard beginning in the morning, afternoon, or evening.

After lunch every other day Delores would go down to the mailroom to check if there was anything in her box. Because of the smallish mailboxes residents were encouraged to check them at least every other day so they wouldn't get too full for the mailman to deal with. The girls were quietly drawing and coloring at one of the tables in the lobby, so Delores didn't think it was necessary to interrupt them.

She planned on doing laundry later that afternoon since the bed bug inspector was on her floor, and he was going to tear apart beds and leave the sheets, comforters, and anything else piled on the floor. Delores, however, had forgotten to tell the girls about him.

The twins paid little mind to Billy Bud when he passed by. They thought he was just one of the residents and gave him a quick "Hi."

He responded with an equally quick "Howdy, girls," as he went by. He had so many apartments to check that he didn't have or take time to do much else. He made his way down the hall and met Norma who came up the stairs from the floor below. They went into Delores' apartment.

The girls needed a potty break. They ran down the hallway and entered their grandma's apartment. They saw Billy Bud in the living room turning a chair over and checking it with a light.

"Who are you and what are you doing in here?" screamed Lucy.

"I'm going to get grandma," yelled Trudy. "She'll call the police on you."

Norma came out of one of the bedrooms when she heard the girls.

"It's OK, it's OK," she yelled just as loud as the girls did.

"Hey girls," said Billy Bud. "Don't let the bed bugs bite."

He laughed but the girls didn't light up at all. They were scared stiff. Delores walked in and realized she had failed to tell the girls that the bed bug inspector would be in the apartment today.

Flabbergasted Delores got a bit mixed up and said, "It's just Billy Bug. He's the bed bud guy."

This caused everyone to laugh and loosened up the girls. While they took turns going to the bathroom, Norma told Delores that there was no evidence of bed bugs and that as soon as Billy Bud was finished in the living room they would leave.

Trudy came back into the living room first. "Why are you looking for bed bugs in the chairs and sofa in here?" she asked. "They aren't called chair bugs or sofa bugs."

"Well," explained Billy Bud, "they latch onto your skin to suck your blood while you're in bed and you carry them into the other rooms when you sit down."

"Yucky," said Lucy who had also come back into the living room. She then started to rub her arms. "I feel all tingly now."

"Let me check you both," said Billy Bud. "Do you have any itchy scabs on you?

"Gross," the girls yelled simultaneously.

Norma, Delores, and Billy Bud all had a good laugh. But not the twins. Norma and Billy Bud continued their journey down the floor and knocked on Dorothy's door next.

12

Dorothy had Parkinson's Disease in its early stages when she first came to the tower. It had shown little, if any, progress over the three years she lived there. Very articulate, she pranced about trim, slim, and full of vim. An athletic lady who wore Indiana University garb, she always watched them play football and basketball on TV ... until recently.

Her aide Macy answered the door. She had been Ethel's aide and worked with seven other residents in the building. In the past year, Dorothy went from barely noticeable symptoms and independent to a slurring, shaking, and unsightly mess who needed a fulltime aide and close supervision.

She had developed a flair for telling stories about herself and didn't care anymore that they contained more falsehoods than truth. It started soon after she added medical marijuana to her daily regime of 13 prescription medications and supplements. Rumors had it, however, that she added more than just the cannabis because of the empty pill bottles that were strewn everywhere in the bathroom that Macy had found when she did an inventory of Dorothy's meds.

In her younger years, as she told over and over, she bragged that she played scratch golf. Captain of both her high school and college golf teams she claimed, although there was no record of her attending school back home in Indiana. She bragged that she played against and beat a young Jack Nicklaus, Tom Weiskopf, and Tony Lema back in the late 1950s in a foursome at an Indianapolis golf course that didn't open until 1974.

Her favorite story, however, centered on her cheerleading prowess. She would start flailing her arms in the lobby and chant a cheer that she said she wrote.

Schellville! Schellville! You are it. SH for Schellville IT for it. Put it all together, and it spells ... Schellville!

She came down to the lobby one morning at 3 a.m. insisting that little fairies and a big monster kept walking across her ceilings and in her walls.

"I can't sleep," she muttered. "There's something or somebody making noise."

Malcolm didn't take her seriously. She even said that she heard one of them in the lobby's bathroom as proof. It turned out, upon investigation by Malcolm, to be he said, "a mop and a broom had fallen, that's all."

Dorothy has a few days of being lucid, but sometimes she is "off her nut," as Macy admitted. She is in a wheelchair and has been for nearly six months. She still yields an old LPGA putter she used as her cane. She wielded it as a knight's lance one recent afternoon to attack Norma singing as if she was Don Quixote.

"What kind of pills are you taking, girl," said Norma not seriously at all.

Dorothy looked long and hard at Norma. She squinted her eyes, furrowed her brow, and hissed. She then turned her wheelchair and zipped away screaming, "I'll get you my pretty, and your little dog, too."

She almost ran into Phillip who was coming around the corner from the mailroom. His balance wasn't what it once was, and Macy grabbed his arm to help steady him.

"Sorry about that," Macy said.

"No harm done little lady," said Phillip. "Hey, Dorothy, how goes it?"

She ignored him and headed straight for the entryway. Macy had to run to catch up to her as the automatic doors opened.

Phillip used to belong to the Arkansas Officials Association when living in Arkansas. He refereed high school football and basketball as well as umpiring both softball and baseball. Mostly he stayed at the high school level, but he did call some youth. On occasion, he got to call junior college games.

He had to retire from this officiating job in 2012 before he reached age 60, however, because he suffered two strokes – one at age 55 and the other at age 59.

The first one, Aphasia, attacked the left side of his brain that controlled communication skills. He taught college history part-time and while in class one September morning his handwriting on the chalkboard slanted down to the right and turned into gibberish, as did his talking. A nursing student in class quickly responded to him by sitting him down and starting to ask him to spell simple words. He could not. She asked him to tell her his phone number. He could not. She called for an ambulance.

In two days at the hospital, he regained most of his skills and the doctor released him from the hospital and sent him home. He took off the rest of the semester. He noticed more sensitivity to sights and sounds, and that he had an inability to multitask. He went back to the classroom in January but felt differently than before, a bit slower and more confused.

His second more severe stroke four years later resulted in Hemiparesis, loss of all motor skills on his right side plus decreased cognitive skills. Phillip bent over to brush off home plate at a high school girls fast-pitch softball game and collapsed. He had to be carried by the EMTs to the ambulance that was called and arrived in under 10 minutes. He spent 14 days rehabbing in the hospital before doctors allowed him to go home.

It took another year for him to graduate from a wheelchair to a walker to a cane to walking slowly unaided. He retired from teaching, too, mostly because his speech slurred and he had many periods of confusion, memory loss, erratic behavior, and hallucinations.

He continued to work at home on his skills despite doctors telling him that what progress he made in a year would be as far as rehabbing would go. When he started having violent outbursts and memory losses, his daughter decided to put him on the waiting lists of all the independent living facilities in the area and the Piedmont Tower had an opening first.

As a moving in gift his daughter Cassie bought him a rollator, told him to walk with it every day, and gave him some sweet pepper seeds to plant in the garden. She visited him almost every Saturday and brought a sack lunch for them to share.

He still has mental difficulties along with his physical limitations. Once he found himself at IHOP at 2:30 in the morning eating a veggie plate and drinking a strawberry milkshake. He told the story to Malcolm one early morning.

"I had no idea how I got there," he said. "I would never order such a combination."

Another time he stood in the parking lot picking up imaginary rocks and swinging an imaginary bat. Yet another incident involved him shooting an imaginary gun all along the rooftop of the west wing of the tower.

Blanche saw him and reported it to the office. "You should have seen him," she said. "He was doing sound effects and cussing a blue streak."

13

Blanche worked as an assistant to JJ Magnifico, a local magician who made appearances all around the area. He performed at birthday parties, club meetings, and retirement homes mostly, but occasionally would earn a gig at casinos or night clubs up to 200 miles away in any direction.

Blanche was 18 in 1997 when she started working for JJ and stayed with him both professionally and personally until 2013 when she became wheelchair bound and had to move to an independent living facility.

Blanche lost her feet to osteomyelitis as massive infections from ulcers resulted in amputation. JJ crafted her a custom wheelchair that earned the name 'BL-mobile.' Its glossy black color with red trim and its wings on the back made it look like the Batmobile of the 1960s TV show.

The twins, Trudy, and Lucy, often hung around the elevators in the lobby waiting for Blanche. They enjoyed riding up to her 10th-floor apartment on the west wing. After they walked Blanche to her apartment the girls would dart into the stairway.

Blanche loved to play penny slots at the local casinos. A group of ladies and men went every Friday night to eat and gamble. They set an hour and a half time limit in the casino after supper and were always back at the tower before 10 p.m.

Blanche had her picture taken with Batman when he came to the casino that she and the others were playing at to promote new Batman slot machines. Blanche and Batman ate supper together at the casino's steakhouse, with the compliments of the management. Batman thrilled Blanche by presenting her with a plaque naming her an honorary citizen of Gotham City and signing the photograph. She also received $50 in free play, also with the compliments of the management, which she used to try out one of the Batman slot machines. She won $28 with Batman and a crowd looking on.

"Extraordinary luck my good citizen," Batman said. "You are indeed fortunate. All of Gotham City salutes you."

She carried the photograph with her until satisfied that all her friends had seen it. She then had it framed and hung it on her apartment door.

She zipped around the walking trails at the tower in her wheelchair, worked in the garden, and usually was one of the first to arrive at the weekly shuffleboard games held outside when weather permitted. She visited friends on all 15 floors and knew about all the gossip that cascaded through the tower.

"Have you heard about ..." was her favorite opening line whenever she talked to anyone.

Blanche loved all the pets and knew them by name. Even the few that weren't dogs or cats. She had names for the feral cats that scampered about outside begging daily for food. She called a smaller and younger mama cat Mumu, her orange brother Soda Pop, a gray domestic shorthair Amazon, a fluffy black male Dakota, and the bigger and older mama cat Spots.

As the summer weather heated up a snake slithered across the grassy field by the picnic areas. She named it Jake. It liked to sun itself on one of the far sidewalks.

"He had a round head and round eyes," observed Blanche. "So, he wasn't venomous."

Soda Pop and Mumu kept a distant eye on him and then enjoyed playing with his molted skin when the time came. Soda Pop would prance around with it in his mouth and Mumu would try to take it away from him.

Blanche during her early morning jaunts, and after she watered her flowers in the garden, would also throw food that Agnes had given her in the pond to feed the fish and the geese.

"There's enough people feeding the cats, but hardly anybody looking after the geese or fish," she would say.

Agnes occupied an apartment on the 10th floor, across the hall and one door down from Blanche. Agnes had been a resident since the tower opened. Almost 100 years old she had white hair that had receded about halfway to the back of her head. Her nose looked like the Wicked Witch of the West. She still walked with her rollator, but with her head down and her back slumped. She always had the right of way because she no longer bothered to watch out where she was going. Besides, her hearing was so bad that she couldn't tell that anyone was hollering at her.

She had taught typing and stenography during the 1950s when typewriters were manual, and secretaries were mostly women. She kept an old mint green Royal typewriter in her apartment as well as a black rotary phone.

Every month a list of residents with birthdays was posted on the bulletin boards. She would send them cards signed with the "yours truly" steno mark. It was a nice gesture but out of character for her other actions.

She knew when the security guards made their rounds. She would wait until they got on the elevator and then go inside their office and rummage through the files and drawers.

Her excuse when caught was, "I lived here before you came. I'll probably still be here after you're gone."

Agnes would move the chairs or decorations in the lobby without asking permission. She insisted that the big mirror hanging between the bathroom doors was two-way and that any bumps on the walls housed tiny cameras that spied on everyone.

Her paranoia manifested itself to the extent that she thought any new residents had wires on and if they wore ball caps, then they had hidden microphones in them. She said to anyone that whenever someone in management used either bathroom in the lobby it signaled to hold secret meetings and to spy behind the two-way mirror.

Like Jean Valjean in *Les Miserables* she took the silver candle sticks from the lounge on her floor because she thought they held secret microphones. She would rub her fingers across the walls of the halls feeling for bumps containing the tiny cameras.

She also had a penchant for taking one of two pieces of any jigsaw puzzle being worked on at one of the lounge tables on her floor and blaming it on the spies who she claimed came at night.

She and Blanche would complain constantly to Mike or Norma about the temperature in the hallway and lounge on their floor. It was always, according to them, either too hot or too cold but never just right.

"I saw Ducky sitting in the lounge the other day. He was wrapped in a blanket," complained Agnes to Norma. "The air conditioning just blows and goes."

"Yeah," sneered Blanche at Norma. "And when the heat is on its way too hot."

14

Dicky, who everyone called Ducky because he weighed 320 pounds and waddled when he walked, couldn't hear very well, and was always angry. To him Ducky just sounded like Dicky and he never caught on, much to the delight of everyone who lived on the 10th floor. Not liked by the management and barely tolerated by his neighbors, he usually smelled like urine and had bad breath.

His thick beard more than made up for his bald head which he rubbed periodically with his right hand. He had recently given up smoking and had another habit of using his left hand to reach into his shirt pocket to grab an imaginary cigarette and pass it on his lips.

He spent much of his mornings almost every day in the lounge on his floor drinking coffee. He couldn't wait for someone to use the vending machines or coffee pot so he could complain about not liking his life, the tower, or current events. He had a penchant for striking up fallacy-filled arguments.

Dicky drove an old pickup truck that made a loud, scratchy sound every time he started it up. Of course, his parking space was near the front door where it could be heard almost all the way up to the top floor. Its brakes squealed and it was always dirty. One could hear the gears grind every time he shifted. In fact, one time someone drew a duck on the dust that gathered on his back window. He never noticed or just didn't care.

He would look out the window every morning and check the sign on the gas station across the street to see if the gas price changed.

"It was $2.79 last week, went up to $2.89 yesterday, and today it's $2.99," he blustered at Millie one morning as she poured a cup of coffee.

"Damn those oil companies for taking advantage of us little folks," he started in. "Why do they keep changing all the time?" he continued. "I'll tell you why."

At this Millie quickly grabbed a sugar packet. She waved and smiled at Dicky. She didn't say anything and only heard "It's the …" as she zoomed around the corner headed back to her apartment.

Millie always wore elastic waist jeans and pulled them up to just under her bosom. She usually had a hair ribbon on her ponytail that matched the main color of her blouse. She had mostly black hair with streaks of gray around her temples. Red canvas shoes with yellow shoestrings completed her look.

She loved to gossip and had Dicky pegged as a leading candidate for having bed bugs because of how much mess he made near the sofa in the lounge. It seemed that bed bugs were always a leading topic of discussion amongst some of the residents. It didn't help matters that flyers on the subject were posted on all the bulletin boards and pamphlets were distributed at least twice a year to each apartment.

She owned a miniature black poodle named Sparky. She would carry the dog in her arms whenever taking it outside instead of putting her in a buggy. Sparky would growl showing her teeth anytime Millie stopped to talk enroute to the dog park. She was not as social as Millie and sometimes would snap if you tried to pet her.

Millie's 23-year-old son Jimmy visited her nearly every day. He was born on Millie's 30th birthday. More like Sparky than Millie, he turned away if you saw him, tried to speak with him, or otherwise crossed paths with him.

Rumors had it from hearing bits and pieces of what Millie sometimes said, she had a habit of changing subjects left and right when talking, that he was not happy that his parent's divorced particularly since his dad married a younger woman less than a year later. Jimmy was 10 at the time and still doesn't talk to his dad.

Myrtle passed Millie in the hall shuffling to the lounge still wearing her red robe and slippers. She wore heavy eye makeup and too much cheap perfume. She needed to walk with a cane but seldom did. She sometimes got her days and nights mixed up.

She bought a honey bun from the vending machine and asked Dicky, "Is it seven in the morning and getting light or seven in the evening and getting dark?"

He didn't look at her but laughed condescendingly. He loved to goad her since he knew she had been a high school civics teacher. He intentionally started a discussion with her about the state legislature. It escalated to include the federal government, the United Nations, abortion rights, and presidential elections.

Dicky admitted to only a couple of years of high school before he dropped out to work in the hardware store owned by his dad.

"I don't need no Shakespeare," he would sometimes say.

He got a bottle of pills out of his shirt pocket, shook out two onto the table, and swallowed them with a swig of his diet Pepsi.

"Yeah, boy," he then said. "Gets me through the day."

Myrtle easily dismantled his fallacious arguments much to his frustration.

"I don't think the United Nations buildings should be in the United States," he said at one point.

Myrtle immediately countered with, "The United Nations is not on United States soil. It is on international territory. It has its own security, fire department, and post office."

"No, it's in Manhattan," Dicky said with an air of authority. "I been there and seen it."

"Yes, it is," Myrtle explained, "but the land after World War II was designated as an international zone."

Dicky quickly changed the subject to discussing his opinions about the electoral college and its role in the first four presidential elections of the 21st century. When Myrtle corrected him that there had only been three presidential elections so far this century, Dicky's frustration turned into anger.

He got red-faced, stood up, and loudly counted, "2000, 2004, 2008, 2012, that's four."

"The new century didn't start until 2001," Myrtle calmly said, "2000 was the last election of the 20th century."

Dicky lost it at this point. As he stomped to his apartment, he said teasingly but firmly, "Am I going to have to shoot you and throw you out of the window?" He then burped loudly.

"Of all the nerve," Myrtle said under her breath as she picked up his empty soda can, brushed the cookie crumbs from the chair where he sat, picked up the newspaper he left on the table, and flung them all in the trash can. She then poured herself a cup of coffee and sat down at the table.

Her reading glasses fell from her nose as she sat down but they caught themselves thanks to the cord she had draped around her neck. A half-finished jigsaw puzzle depicting a bunch of colorful cupcakes lay on the table. She worked on it for half an hour filling in 20 pieces. Concentrating on the puzzle she didn't hear the noises coming from the stairwell behind the vending machines. Myrtle's phone rang and it was Hazel calling to see if she was awake.

"Wakey, wakey," said Hazel, "Are you up?"

"Yes. I am," said Myrtle. "I'm in the lounge working on a puzzle and drinking coffee."

"Well, come on down," invited Hazel, "I've made cranberry muffins."

15

Hazel lived near the middle of the second floor just above the bathrooms in the lobby. Widowed for over 18 years, she had an aging cat named Bullwinkle. She would joke that she replaced her "dearly departed" with the cat.

Hazel had no teeth, long brown hair, and stood over 6 feet tall. She weighed only 120 pounds. Her clothes hung on her. She always had on maroon fingernail polish and her too thick lipstick matched its color.

She walked a mile every morning and every night, occasionally taking time to feed the fish stocked in the pond. She would tear pieces of lettuce and throw it to them.

Hazel also grew roses in her garden plot. They always bloomed prettier and thicker than anyone else's thanks, she said, because of her unique way of planting them. She would ask the others who grew tomatoes to give her any of them that weren't quite nice enough to keep. She would cut them in half, plug sprigs from rose bushes that she picked the thorns off, and plant them in pots. Six weeks later, they would have richly colored blooms bigger and nicer than anyone else. At night when Hazel couldn't sleep, she would cuss and fuss at her walls, ceiling, and floor.

"I'm getting really pissed off," was her favorite thing to say and it, along with whatever else she yelled, could be heard by neighbors in the apartments adjacent and across the hall from her.

Invariably Hazel would leave her apartment by slamming the door, marching to the elevators, and when the doors opened in the lobby, charging the late-night security guard, usually Malcolm, with her complaint that "there must be rats the size of people crawling around."

Malcolm would smirk, try hard not to laugh out loud at her, and tell her that it was probably just the water pipes from the bathrooms below her gurgling and draining.

"This property is over 35 years old," he'd say.

Hazel would usually put her hands on her hips and stare at Malcolm with squinting eyes.

"I'll report it," he always said at that point to appease her.

"Just wait until one of those monstrous critters eats its way through the walls," she warned. "Bullwinkle and I won't have a chance."

Malcolm would fix her a cup of coffee and talk about recipes until she calmed down.

She would then usually go outside to smoke a cigarette, take a walk, and stop by the garden for a quick check of her plants. On her way back in she would sit on a bench and listen to birds.

Hazel used to work as a waitress at a fancy restaurant in the southwest corner of Indiana where the Ohio and Wabash rivers met. Located almost under an old bridge over the Wabash River that had recently been converted to a pedestrian crossing, the restaurant had its own gardens from which the salads were made and raised the cattle on site for their steaks. Hazel learned her tricks for gardening and cooking from those years working there.

She loved to tell the others who gardened to "sprinkle baking soda in the dirt around your vegetable plants when they first start to bloom to make them taste sweeter."

When Myrtle made it down to Hazel's apartment, she was introduced to Harv and Suzanne who had started having coffee and eating cranberry muffins.

16

Harv and Suzanne, one of those couples that almost everyone instantly took a comfortable liking to, moved into their 10th floor apartment at the end of the west wing.

Hazel claimed it was cursed. "The previous four couples who occupied that apartment had one of them die within ten months of moving into it – three men and one woman," Hazel told.

"Just a coincidence," said Myrtle. "Shame on you for bringing it up," she said sarcastically scolding Hazel.

Harv and Suzanne didn't know this at the time they moved in, but other stories, usually told by Dicky, soon gravitated to them about the speculation. When the man in the apartment next to them died within a month of Harv and Suzanne moving in, the gossip escalated.

"I told you so," said Dicky. "I just knew something would happen."

Harv caught the covid soon after moving in. He and Suzanne had to be quarantined for three weeks. Everyone who knew about the curse of the apartment didn't expect to ever see them again.

When Harv emerged, 16 pounds lighter, with a bigger bald spot than before, and on a rollator instead of a cane, everyone concerned felt relieved but a bit hesitant toward approaching him the same way, especially Dicky.

"I'm not going to have anything to do with them," Dicky said.

Suzanne had only mild symptoms and fared much better than Harv, thanks to always wearing a mask and taking plenty of meds early and often during his ordeal. She always tested negative.

What helped them reestablish their status among the residents, except for Dicky, was that they spent a lot of time outside walking or working in the garden and were sensitive toward the feral clutter of cats. They planted mostly white periwinkles and assorted colors of Gerber daisies. Suzanne sprinkled cayenne pepper around the borders of their plot to keep the cats out.

"I love you babies but stay out of my flowers," she would say to them when they came around.

Harv and Suzanne had been together over 50 years. They first started dating in high school and had been a team ever since. They went to college in Stillwater together and married the same day as commencement. They graduated in the morning and married in the evening.

Avid Oklahoma State Cowboys fans, they still drove to every home football game and weekend home basketball game. Both their kids graduated from OSU.

While taking walks, Harv and Suzanne would call the cats and drop handfuls of dry food near several of the culverts in which the cats went in and out. With each passing week the cats would come closer to them, but not to where they could reach down to pet them. Although Suzanne could almost pet Mumu.

Harv and Suzanne started a weekly game night and before long it grew to where they had three tables of dice, cards, and board games in one of the small rec rooms. There were two pool tables and a ping-pong table in the other small rec. room across the hall and anyone who didn't want to play at the game tables went there and stayed usually until 'lights out.'

Agatha, a mean-spirited woman did like, however, to shoot pool, usually eight ball. She was delightful when winning but not so much when losing, which was seldom.

She would "cuss like a drunken sailor when losing" as Harv would say, "but, purr like a kitten when winning."

Agatha looked more like an old man than a woman. She had a burr haircut, usually wore a red ball cap, never had on any makeup, and dressed in jeans and red sweatshirts. She wore canvas basketball high top gym shoes that she bragged about being over 30 years old.

She always complained about the elevators smelling, going too slowly, and not having bulletin boards. She didn't like the idea of bulletin boards only being in the three laundry rooms located on the first, eighth, and 15th floors.

"We all take the elevators a heck of a lot more than we wash laundry," she would say. "Why can't we put notices there, by gosh."

She also complained that chocolate donuts were not served on 'coffee and donuts' day, usually scheduled for the second Tuesday of every month.

"I don't like plain donuts," she would fuss. "I want chocolate, you hear."

It did no good for Mike to explain to her that if they ordered special donuts for her then they would have to order special for anyone else. Agatha did manage to talk Mike into having the fast-food restaurant that catered lunch on the last day of every month to not add salt to the French fries.

Agatha was best friends with Ethel and like Pearl had a hard time for several months dealing with her death, especially the way it happened.

"She was so careful with her oxygen," Agatha lamented, "She never smoked in her apartment."

Agatha lived across the hall from Delores and didn't like Trudy or Lucy, especially when they met in the elevators. She would pinch them and accuse them of making too much noise.

"You both will end up in jail if you don't start to settle down," she would warn them. "I'm going to tell your mother so."

The girls would hover together as far away as they could get in the elevator. They both would turn their backs and face the wall until Agatha got off. They would then run as fast as they could to the opposite stairway and stay quiet until they figured it safe to come out.

Agatha was a bitter woman. She maintained her good health and appearance until her husband had a massive stroke in 2003. She was not ready to be his caregiver and let herself go when he took up all her time and energy. He lived 10 years as an invalid, and she just wore out.

Ethel encouraged her to move into Piedmont and even though three other places called first with openings, Agatha opted to hold out to be with her old friend Ethel who was going downhill quickly. It didn't last long, though.

Agatha had a smoking buddy Amelia that she spent most of her time with. They went outside to the smoking area together at least 10 times a day and night. Neither one of them could sleep much, and nighttime was just the same to them as daytime.

Another thing they had in common was their dislike for animals. They wouldn't get on the elevator if someone was already in there with their dog. They never talked to or petted any of them. Big or small, they ignored them.

They had the same disdain for cats, whether they were pets of residents or any of the feral clutter that ran about. They didn't like that piles of food would be left for them and wished they would just go away.

"Shoo, mangy things," Amelia would yell at them. "Go back where you came from."

"I wish people would stop feeding them," echoed Agatha.

17

Will had a curious manner about him, probably from being a police detective for over 38 years. Now 70 years old and in a wheelchair, he decided to write a book to keep himself busy at nights when he couldn't sleep, a behavior that only started when he moved into the tower.

His days of playing golf with his son, working in the yard with his wife who recently divorced him, and coaching youth softball with his daughter had ended. He had to fill his time with activities that pretty much kept him inside his apartment at the retirement community.

He was having a hard time adjusting to being in a wheelchair and incapable of doing a lot of the things he had taken for granted that he would still be able to do during his retirement years. He spent hours on his computer playing online golf, free slots, and word games. He watched all the airplane movies and 1950s monster movies on the TV. He worked on jigsaw puzzles either of dogs, cats, cottages, or bridges.

He ate mostly a protein diet of fried round steak. He drank way too many diet sodas. Mostly, though, he enjoyed his writing and watching the feral cats. He often looked out his windows to see if they were out. It pleased him to see a clutter of them roaming the premises and that several residents kept them fed. He spent time in the dog and cat parks, too, petting any of them that would let him.

He started writing soon after he moved in but was having a hard time fleshing out any of his ideas. When he began hearing all the tales the residents told him while he spent time outside during the early mornings or late evenings, he got an idea. Talking with them while wandering around the trails inspired him. He started anew and the words started flowing like water from a hose. He finally came up with a concept and began writing about a love triangle centered around a drug deal at a BBQ joint just off the interstate highway in New Mexico. This gave him a reason to keep busy and it improved his mood.

Gossiping more accurately described the conversations he had, but it led Will to chat with most of the residents, the subject of some of the stories he would fictionize for his book. He tried to not make it seem like a detective interviewing witnesses when he talked to the residents, but he was what he was.

It started with Agatha and her insistence that Ethel never smoked in her apartment.

"She didn't even have any ashtrays," Agatha said. "She knew it was too dangerous with her oxygen equipment."

Will, the retired resident, became Will, the curious detective, and he wanted to know more about Ethel's time at the tower.

"Well," Agatha started, "she and Bill the property manager back then were friends until she got sick right after her husband died. Then she started fussing at him about a lot of things. They had a falling out."

"What kind of falling out?" asked Will, trying not to get too much into his detective mode.

"She went to the owners once too often about her fear of somebody stealing all her jewelry," Agatha said while getting more exasperated. "She just stopped wearing it all and wanted to keep it in a safe in her bedroom closet."

"What kind of jewelry did she have?" Will grew more interested.

"A diamond necklace, earrings, and a ring," said Agatha. "Oh, she was so proud of them. She used to be in pageants, you know, and she was married to a cop, too."

Will was a young officer on the team Herb led that busted the drug ring back in 1977.

"I knew Herb well," said Will. "I always looked up to him, but he changed after the drug bust."

"Cocaine and heroin, Ethel used to tell me the story often," said Agatha.

"And lots of opioid pills, too," Will added.

"Oh, I didn't realize," a surprised Agatha said.

"Why was she so afraid?" asked Will.

Agatha didn't answer and the interview promptly ended when she said, "I don't want to say any more about it."

Will found this a bit disturbing but moved on to Agnes. Despite her being almost 100 years old and wanting to talk about her dog, she offered some interesting input about Bill between her tales about her poodle 'Happy Chappy.' She didn't want to talk about Ethel, either.

"Bill and I both lived in New York," she said. "I know the hotel where he worked." She then leaned forward and whispered, "something happened but I don't remember."

"Tell me the name of the hotel and I can look it up," a curious Will said. "It might be on its website."

"I read about it in the paper," Agnes remembered as she picked up 'Happy Chappy.' "It was on the TV, too."

"What was the name of the hotel?" Will asked again.

"It was the Vendome."

These two conversations led Will to forget about his book writing for now and to concentrate, instead, on the feeling he had on the back of his neck. As had been the case for years, goosebumps caused him to rub the hair there, a sign that something intrigued him about what Agatha and Agnes had said, and what they didn't say. Something beyond just fodder for a book.

"So much for just being an old man," thought Will. "I guess I'll go with this." A part of him was excited about having detective work to do again, but part of him wanted to just write and lead an otherwise boring life without much drama.

18

Sure enough, with just a little Internet research, Will found out that a series of robberies occurred at Hotel Vendome the Summer of Sam in New York City. During the black outs, seven apartments reported break ins. Nobody was ever arrested, and it remained a mystery. Will found this odd, and it prompted him to call New York that afternoon.

The Vendome, once a four-star hotel, had since been converted into apartments and fallen into disarray with "more cats and rats than paying customers," admitted Sal, the manager, as he talked on his cell phone to Will.

"Can you tell me anything about the robberies back in '77?" Will asked.

"I don't know about that," Sal said. "I wasn't even born yet. But the doorman back then is still around."

"I guess you can't tell me his name or where I might get a hold of him," Will said more out of habit than really expecting anything other than "no."

"Sure, I can," beamed Sal. "He lives in the attic and owes, by the way, three-month rent."

Will could hear caterwauling in the background, the yells of people arguing, and doors slamming.

"His name is Al and I'll have him call you when he comes down to get his cup of coffee this afternoon," Sal had to yell to be heard over all the ruckuses. "I got your number in my phone."

Finding this out Will, now in full detective mode, decided to contact Bill in Florida to get his firsthand information about Al and the hotel robberies. He got Bill's cell phone number from Mike, as well as the number and address of the retirement village they listed. It took some coaxing, but Mike let him have the information about Bill. Will won out after telling him what he had found out.

"Once a cop, always a cop," he said in his best 'bad cop' intimidating voice and matching facial expression.

He called Bill's cell phone several times but got no answer. He called the number of the retirement village. The manager and his assistant both reported that they had never heard of Bill or Gladys.

Will immediately told Mike about this. He asked that a meeting be called with the tower owners, board members, all management-level personnel, and security guards.

Gossip and rumors ran rampant among the nosiest of the residents. Norma was placed in charge of quelling them. Her quiet manner and nonplussed attitude would make the residents feel assured nothing too strange was going on. But it didn't take long for the worst-case scenario to surface.

Will started the closed-door meeting with the tower's officials. As he began his cell phone rang.

"New York calling back," he said. "Excuse me, but it's important to take this."

"Is this Will the Okie from Muskogee?" the gravelly voice on the other end bellowed. "Are you living on Tulsa time?"

Al looked as disheveled as the hotel had dilapidated. His jeans had holes and stains. His undershirt had turned a dingy gray from its beginnings of white. His stubble and balding hair looked unkept. His teeth, what there were of them, matched the yellow stain of the two fingers of his left hand where he held his cheap cigars.

When Al stopped laughing at his Oklahoma references Will identified himself, told of the connection to Bill, and asked him if he remembered '77.

"I surely do, yes indeed, you bet," he said. "The Summer of Sam, the black outs because of the heat, and the robberies here at the Vendome. Quite a time."

"Tell me about Bill," Will interrupted.

"He was just back from Vietnam and worked hard, mighty hard, all the time," remembered Al. "We were good friends who really hit it off."

"Tell me about the robberies," Will said thinking that Al was about to share unrelated stories about Bill and him.

"He always wandered about to make sure everything met with his approval; the mini-grocery store, the fitness center, the laundry room, the pool area, even the pet park out back," recalled Al. "But the robberies didn't seem to bother him too much."

"Anything else you can tell me?" Will hoped.

"Oh, just that he liked to go on the roof with his little gal Gladys," Al started laughing. "He was really in love with her."

As Al spoke Will could hear meowing. "I spend time up there now. Just me and the cats."

"I'm a cat person, too." Will admitted. "How many do you have?"

"I don't really have them. They just hang around because of the mice and rats," Al laughed some more. "There's about a dozen or so."

"Do you feed them?" Will asked.

"Don't need to. They eat all the critters," Al laughed again. "Fat and happy."

"I really must be going," Will said as he realized he had a roomful of folks waiting. "I may need to call you back."

"Sooner than later, Cowboy, or is your last name Rogers," Al laughed louder as he hung up, proud of his bevy of Oklahoma references.

Will turned back to the meeting. "The reason I called you here this afternoon, I have a feeling about this Ethel business."

"You don't think it was an accident," Norma blurted. "That's it, isn't it?"

"Yes, that's right," Will said while nodding his head. "I suspect foul play."

"Do you know, who, why, and how?" asked Malcolm.

"One step at a time," he advised as he put out his hand. "I need to talk with a lot more people before I can put this all together."

"A murder mystery," laughed Norma. "That should liven things up around here."

"Well," cautioned Will, "We'll see if that possibility pans out."

"I always thought it kind of shady," said Norma. "I'm glad you're going to look into it."

Will thanked Malcolm for coming in for a meeting in the middle of the day as well as the weekend security guards who also attended.

19

Will made a list of the residents he still wanted to interview. He then zipped through the lobby in his wheelchair to go outside to think. He felt he had pieces of a puzzle but couldn't fit them together yet. Something about Agatha and Agnes not wanting to talk too much about Ethel, and Bill and Gladys lying about going to Florida.

Three cats that had congregated under a Crepe Myrtle tree next to the front doors ran off when Will came out with his wheelchair whirring. He recognized the cats because he had seen them before when he looked out his bedroom window. They would often be romping in the field. There were the three of them as far as he could tell, a bigger girl, a smaller girl, and an orange long-legged boy. Will enjoyed watching them. When he went outside, he would leave a handful of dry food which he called 'crunchies' for them.

Will wasn't the only one who fed and paid attention to the cats. Beatrice, a mother hen of a woman who stuck her nose in everybody's business, would sometimes cut up hamburger or round steak she had fried and leave it in small piles in the bushes. Sometimes she would just throw pieces of cut up hot dogs at the cats. She would let everybody know that any cats should be fed in the bushes away from the parking lot.

"I don't want them to get used to being up here and then getting in the engine of any cars during cold weather," she said. "They jump in there where its warm."

Will quickly joined the "cat people" throng and would keep a bag of dry food in his wheelchair basket in case he saw them.

"I feed them over by the picnic area," Will acknowledged to Beatrice. "Usually a handful of crunchies."

Beatrice when she visited the smoking area several times a day and night, would call the cats with a high-pitched, "Here, kitty, kitty, kitty." That would often get their attention but lure them only if they heard her dropping dry food nearby.

G. L., who walked every morning, would leave some cans of soft food at various locations along the back of walking trails away from the parking lot. After he passed by the cats would sometimes scurry to eat as much as they could before he came around again.

One night from his bedroom window Will heard a screeching cat down below. When he looked, he saw the bigger female being chased by a gray male on the prowl. She wanted nothing to do with the aggressive tomcat no matter how determined he chased her.

Will texted his daughter Sadie, also a cat person who owned two herself, about the incident. She showed up the next afternoon with a trap to hopefully catch the bigger female and take her to the animal shelter to get her spayed, if it wasn't too late.

Sadie brought cut up hot dogs to help lure the cat into the trap. It worked. An excited G.L. let Will know right away by loudly knocking on his door and shouting, "You got a cat in the trap, it's the bigger female."

Will tried to figure out who was who. He surmised that she must have been the mother of the smaller female because they looked so much alike. The smaller female probably was the mother or sister of the orange boy, who now had grown bigger than her.

Will texted Sadie and she came back right away. She took the cat home and let her have the run of the garage for the night. To feel safe in her new but temporary environment, the cat alternated between getting as high as she could on the garage door edge or hiding by crouching behind the dryer vent in the far corner.

The next morning after being lured out from behind the dryer with a can of tuna, Sadie picked up the cat, got her in the carrier, put her in the backseat of her car, and took her to the vet. She meowed all the way just as she had done the night before in the car.

The cat had a "spa day"; spayed, cleaned, shots, and thoroughly checked out. Sadie brought her home for a day of recuperating and then let her loose that evening back at the tower. Luckily, she wasn't pregnant again. She had somehow fended off the advances of the gray male. Thanks to Sadie, the bigger female would no longer be contributing to the clutter or getting chased again by the gray male.

The 'cat people' congratulated Sadie and Will for their efforts. All seemed under control until a gray female cat not of the feral colony showed up and started jumping in the laps of anyone having her. Those who went outside to sit whether in chairs, rollators, or wheelchairs welcomed her into the fold. She would purr, offer a silent meow, and ask for pets. Rumors swelled that someone had dumped her because of her sweet personality and attraction to laps. The next time Will and Sadie talked on the phone he told her about the new arrival.

"I hope she's not pregnant," Will said.

"I bet she is," Sadie added. "Why would anybody dump such a friendly cat if she wasn't."

Will and Sadie took a liking to her. After being trapped by the smell of a can of tuna, the gray girl just like the bigger female spent the night in Sadie's garage, had a "spa day," recuperated a day, and was let loose at the tower.

Her surgery, however, was a bit more intense. She was indeed pregnant. The vet had to abort four kittens. He told Sadie that the cat, only about six months old, was about two weeks from giving birth and probably dumped because of that.

"People don't get their female cats spayed in time," he said. "They dump them, and a feral colony begins."

Free from her kittens and spayed, she spent most of her time thereafter by the front door of the tower quietly wanting to come indoors. She was not a member of the feral cat family, so she hoped for more human intervention. She silently meowed and would try to come into the lobby every time the door opened to let someone in or out. Even the barking of dogs who saw her didn't scare her away.

Paul, one of the daytime security guards, took her home to join his roommate Addie, their playful collie dog Rebel, and their other cat, an aging boy named Crusher. She finally had a 'forever home.' Addie named her Sweetness.

It was now time for Sadie to try and capture the smaller female and have her spayed. She and Will spent a whole week of mornings trying to lure her into the trap. On a Saturday evening when Will went out to zip around the building, he saw the smaller female in the trap. He called Sadie and the process repeated itself for the third time. The cat spent Sunday in Sadie's garage, went for a 'spa day' on Monday at the vet, recuperated back at Sadie's, and was set free at the tower that evening.

All the female cats had now been spayed and Sadie decreed, "that should be the end of the feral colony growing."

All this cat business distracted Will from his unofficial investigation into Ethel's demise, but it led to another oddity only a week later. When he went outside, he noticed the smaller female and the orange boy frantically digging along the foundation on the west side of the tower. He had been told by Blanche that the bigger female was called Spots, the smaller female Mumu, and the orange boy Soda Pop.

20

There were still more residents to talk with. Will wanted to know, particularly, about Pearl and her stories about the sounds she insisted belonged to her dead husband and Dorothy's insistence that fairies frequented her ceilings and walls.

Pearl met Will for their talks in the lounge. She wouldn't let him in her apartment. She offered each time to buy him a soft drink and a candy bar from the vending machines, but he always declined.

During one of their visits she mentioned, quite innocently to her, but fascinatingly to Will, that she heard scratches, and she assumed Bert's footsteps on his way to visit her.

"He comes up the stairway and goes right into the bedroom," she said. "I don't even know when he comes in the front door."

Will saw Dorothy one afternoon with her aide Macy outside sitting at one of the picnic tables. They watched and listened to the birds, particularly a mockingbird that chirped loudly from a Bradford Pear tree. It seemed to relax Dorothy even though she shook and lurched in her wheelchair due to her Parkinson's.

Will thought to himself that even though he sat in a wheelchair, he wasn't as bad off as Dorothy. He felt bad that he often complained about his knees and back, but he could get up and down, and he could even walk a short distance with his cane. He was lucid most of the time but admittedly had bad mental days on occasion.

As he asked Dorothy a question about her fairies, Macy suggested they go to her apartment and eat supper while they talked. Macy, a big girl with long salt and pepper hair that went all the way down her back, quickly started pushing Dorothy toward the front door.

Will, who took Lasix every day, knew what was going on and said, "I'll be there in a few minutes."

Macy mouthed, "thank you," and away they went. Will used the time to also use the bathroom in the lobby.

While Macy cooked, Dorothy told her stories about the noises in her apartment in between talking randomly about the Indianapolis 500 race. She bragged that she came in third as the person singing *"Back Home Again in Indiana"* with the TV personality Mike Rowe coming in second.

"He and I had dinner at Bigelow after our audition," she recounted. "We had the best Kielbasa and signed autographs until almost closing time."

Will remembered from going to conventions that Bigelow was an old German restaurant famous for its draft beers, but that it was in Chicago, not Indianapolis. He brushed it off having a hard time also believing about her fairies. But something told him to file her stories away just like jigsaw puzzle pieces that go back in the box because they don't fit together yet.

They ate a salmon patty on a whole wheat bun, pickled beets, and fried potatoes with onions. Will put mustard on his patty and ketchup on his potatoes. He ate four beets and chugged down a glass of sweet tea.

Dorothy continued to intersperse her answers to Will's questions with more tales from her imagined days in Indiana. He particularly enjoyed hearing her bragging incoherently and inconsistently about being a special assistant coach one season for Indiana University's basketball team.

Dorothy joined the list of residents with similar stories that led Will to think there must be something or someone creeping around the walls of the tower. Hazel added her piece to the puzzle.

She had the garden plot next to Will's and kept an eye on it since he wasn't mobile enough to really take care of it as it needed. He had planted some marigolds in a pot that were doing well but needed help from Hazel to plant rows of green beans. She watered them for him.

During one of the mornings that Will visited the garden area, Hazel told him about her "rats." She insisted that she heard them crawl around.

"I think they are coming from the bathrooms below me," she said quite emphatically. "I hear them in the walls and floor."

"You're not the only person that says they hear noises," Will said. "This place is, what, over 35 years old?"

To change the subject, Hazel asked Will about the cats outside. She had recently lost her cat Bubbles who was 21 years old. She doubted that she would get another cat for fear that it would outlive her. Will obliged and eagerly told her about what had happened just a few nights before.

"Phillip, Harv, and I love to talk about dogs and cats," his story began.

They spend time outside during the cool nights when hardly anyone else stirs about. Besides, they hope cats will be out, too.

"Sure enough, one night here comes the smaller female and the orange boy," Will continued as Hazel leaned forward on her chair that she kept near her garden plot.

"Mumu and Soda Pop," she said.

"They would flank us about ten feet away. Waiting to be fed, they would sit patiently until I dropped some dry food and it hit the sidewalk. We would get a safe distance from them of about 10 feet before we would stop and turn around to see if they were eating yet. The bigger female came from around the corner and joined the feeding frenzy."

"That would be Spots," Hazel added.

"But what happened next surprised us. Two kittens popped out from the bushes. They looked like the big gray tomcat that came to visit and conduct business with the bigger female, uh Spots," continued Will. "Mumu and Soda Pop apparently had baby-sitting duty and they protected the kittens while they ate. They had dark gray fur, short legs, and big heads like the gray tomcat that we assumed was their daddy."

"Oh my," said Hazel. She got up and continued to water her garden plot.

"After eating a play session took place," continued Will. "The kittens pounced on each other, wrestled, and yelped pitifully much to our amusement. A few minutes later they all scurried into the bushes. The kittens, a bit clumsily, though."

"They are so cute," Hazel said. "Too bad someone here doesn't take any of them in."

"We decided the kittens needed naming," Will went on with his story. "Since we didn't know the kittens' gender, we decided on names describing their dark fur color – Raven and Shadow."

"You better check with Blanche," Hazel laughed. "She names all the critters, you know."

21

Will didn't know what to expect when he moved into the tower, but he soon found out.

"Colorful people," he thought to himself. "Lots of stories about them. Feral cats to keep an eye on, too."

But he never thought the possibility of murder would welcome him as he began his retirement years. While he wasn't quite as sharp as he used to be in his prime, he believed he had enough of his senses to eventually figure out this puzzle. After all he was learning the names of all the pet dogs and cats and keeping them separate from the names of the residents he met.

If he still worked for the city, and wasn't wheelchair bound, he would go to New York and Florida to follow leads but now he must use his cell phone and computer.

He often described himself as being, "B+ mentally and D- physically."

He was still a handsome man with white hair now that matched the color of his moustache. He tried to comb his hair back off his forehead, but it seemed to always fall forward a bit. He had gained over 40 pounds in recent years, but he carried it well. He had little to no fashion sense, however, often wearing plaid Bermuda shorts with flowered Hawaiian shirts. At least he didn't wear socks with his sandals and his colors usually matched, sort of.

Some residents, like Will, used wheelchairs. Some used rollators, some used canes, and some were in various stages of walking unaided. They all ranged in age from 60 to 100. Some had been living in the tower since it opened, and some were 'newbies.' Will considered himself one of them since he had only been a resident for seven months. Long enough, though, to make a snarky observation to his daughter.

"It's like a junior high school only a lot grayer, wackier, and more wrinkled."

But one thing seemed consistent enough about the many stories, no matter how wacky they sounded, that Will began to think there might be more to the tower building than meets the eye, which gave him an idea.

He went outside, wheeled across the street about 100 yards from the building, and looked at the tower to see if anything seemed off-kilter. Nothing looked uneven to him, but still he had the sneaking suspicion that there was something strange about the interior of the building.

Will talked to the Harmon's about the construction of the tower. They told him he would find out everything about it by searching 'property records' online. Glad he didn't have to venture downtown to look through files like in the old days, he sat at his computer in his apartment and found all sorts of information that would have taken days and many trips to the courthouse, library, and the offices of builders and engineers.

Will found out the building had been renovated and updated in 2002 when the original owner died, and his son inherited the property. The blueprints matched the actual layout. It all checked out, but Will still had a feeling the blueprints didn't show everything. He needed to talk with the builders. They, unfortunately, were no longer alive and their business didn't exist anymore. Mysteriously, they hadn't kept complete or organized files.

Will looked at the tower from all angles. He even asked Phillip and G.L. to look, too. They all came to the same conclusion. The tower had two equal wings slightly angled. Front, sides, and back all looked the same. Will, however, remained skeptical.

Finally, with permission from the owners who agreed to take care of the cost, Will contacted surveyors to measure the tower. They did and what they found out confirmed his suspicions. The west wing stood 2.8 feet longer and 2.8 feet higher than the east wing. Not enough to be detectable by the naked eye, but enough to show up on the surveyors' instruments.

Will told these results to the owners, board members, and management. A combination of shock and confusion led to questions from them.

"What does this mean?"

"Is the building sinking on one side?"

"Are the apartments on the west side bigger than the east side?"

Will put up both his hands to quiet the gathering. "Don't you see, the west wing probably has a passageway along the wall and ceiling."

"Oh my God," said Gertrude, "I never ..."

Will cut her off and explained that this seemed to confirm for him what the residents on that side of the tower had been saying.

"They aren't as crazy as they sound," he told them.

He mentioned, for example, Pearl's claims of visits from her dead husband, Dorothy's fairies on the ceiling, and Agnes's suspicions.

"You see," he began, "there's probably a crawl space somehow on that end of the building."

"So, Ethel might have been killed by accident," said Mike.

"Or murdered by someone who used the crawl space," added Norma.

"Don't jump to any conclusions just yet," said Will. "I intend to find out, but I have my suspicions."

22

Every Sunday afternoon Will's daughter Sadie came over to spend the afternoon with him. They visited with any dogs or cats if any of them were out. On this one Sunday while sitting outside watching for any cats to trot by, Will told her about the smaller female Mumu and the orange boy Soda Pop digging a hole by the west wing foundation.

Sadie decided she should investigate. Will couldn't navigate the bushes and rocky terrain of the landscaped area between the sidewalk and the building, so he had to stay where he was. Sadie managed not to fall as she walked amongst the shrubs and rocks all the way to the wall. But startled when she got there by the two kittens, Raven, and Shadow, who came out from the hole, Sadie yelped and fell into a Spirea bush. This caused the two kittens to scamper away and try to climb one of the nearby small Willow trees.

When Sadie composed herself and looked closer at the hole, she saw two shiny objects in the dirt. She dug just a little bit and dragged out what looked like diamonds.

"Oh my gosh," she yelled. "Look what I found."

She ran to Will and handed them to him. He couldn't believe it either.

"Oh my, what's this?" He said while brushing off the dirt and inspecting the stones.

"Are they real?" Sadie asked.

"I don't know, but I know ways to maybe find out." Will added.

Using a couple of tricks, he had learned during his years as a detective, he first blew his breath on the stones. They didn't get foggy. That led him to believe they might be real. Next, he asked Sadie to go inside and get a glass of water. When he dropped the stones in the glass they fell to the bottom.

"I think they are real," he said. "But these two tests don't prove anything yet. We need to show them to a jeweler to be sure."

"What on earth did you just do?" Sadie asked while wrinkling up her face.

"Well, real diamonds won't stay foggy when you breathe on them like glass does," Will took off his glasses and breathed on them to show her. "See how the fog takes a few seconds to go away."

"What does the water show?" She then asked.

"Glass will usually float or sink more slowly, and diamonds will sink right away because they have more density," he said. "But we need to be sure."

"Do you know any jeweler?" Sadie excitedly asked.

"Yes, I do," said Will. "Let's go back up to my apartment and I'll call her."

Will called Sally McNair, a jeweler and old friend of the police force. He told her the story. So enamored with it she volunteered to come over that evening to verify his initial findings.

Will and Sadie needed to kill time, so they raided his refrigerator. They ate a dinner of sliced barbecue chicken sandwiches, potato salad, and baked beans. They then worked on a jigsaw puzzle getting all the end pieces fit together. Finally, about 6:30 Sally arrived. Taking out her loupe for closer inspection she studied the nuggets closely and pronounced them as real diamonds.

"Are there anymore?" she asked. "These are really nice."

"I don't know," said Will. "Let's go and see."

Will and Sadie took Sally outside to show her where the cats had dug the hole. She felt around with her hands for a few seconds and then pulled out a necklace.

"Oh my," she said while blowing and brushing off the dirt. "What have we here?" She showed what she found to Will and Sadie.

"Well, I'll be," said Will. He didn't say anything else to Sadie or Sally, but he figured the necklace might have belonged to Ethel. He remembered what

Agatha had said about her jewelry, but he couldn't figure out how the necklace got all the way to the ground from the 15th floor.

He asked Sally to make a quick estimate about how much the diamonds in the necklace were worth. It looked like two were missing from the strand, most likely the ones Sadie had found.

"Well," she figured. "There are 10 of them all together."

"So how much do you think?" asked Will.

"Each one is pea sized which is about a carat, and the going price is $2,000," she surmised.

"Wow," said Sadie, "That necklace is worth $2,000. Holy cow."

"No, no," laughed Sally. "Each diamond is worth $2,000."

Sadie gasped but said nothing. She couldn't.

"You better let me have it," said Will. "I need to show it to Mike tomorrow. It will help with what I plan to tell him."

Sally gave the necklace to Will. He handed it and the two loose diamonds to Sadie.

"You carry it all up to my apartment," he said. "Some cat toy, eh!"

Gob smacked, Sadie trembled and started walking carrying the necklace like it was a glass full of water that couldn't be spilled. Will and Sally looked at each other and laughed quietly.

First thing Monday morning Will met with Mike. He showed him the diamonds, told him where they were found, and that they were valued at about $20,000. Mike was stunned.

Will told Mike that he figured the most logical explanation was for the extra space along the side and top of the west wing to be just enough for a crawl space.

"Someone knew about it and used it to get into Ethel's apartment," Will deduced. "They took the jewelry, killed Ethel, made it look like an accident, and during the escape dropped the necklace. It fell all the way down to the ground and the cats somehow dug it up."

Mike leaned back in his chair and shook his head. "That's pretty wild."

"But it makes sense once you put all the pieces together," Will said.

"You were the detective," Mike sighed. "My gosh."

"I think there is more to it, though," said Will. "I think she was distributing pills, too."

"Who, Ethel?" Mike asked.

"Yes, and I think she had help," added Will. "We must find access to the crawl space."

Mike suggested Harv to help him find the entry. Will thought it a good idea because he would be no good on the stairways where they agreed the access must be. They also agreed that they must tell Harv the whole story to get him to go along with helping. When they did, he insisted on seeing the hole by the foundation, the diamonds, and the view from across the street of the uneven wings.

"I don't see any difference in the two wings," Harv said.

"Well, there is, the surveyors proved it with their equipment," Will insisted.

"Let's go back in and find it," Mike said slightly on edge. "If it's there."

"Oh, it's there all right," Will insisted as he wheeled away.

They started with the stairway in the lobby and scrutinized all the way up to the 10th floor with no luck. It took almost all day of knocking on walls, stomping on steps, and poking on ceilings.

The next morning, they continued up to the 15th floor but couldn't find anything. Tired and frustrated by noon, Mike suggested that they eat lunch in the kitchen. Two maintenance men having sack lunches were watching the TV located on the wall at the far end of the kitchen. A James Bond movie *You Only Live Twice* was about to play.

Mike made Will and Harv ham and cheese sandwiches. He also got out from his stash in the refrigerator some Cole slaw and sweet pickles. They each got a can of soda from the vending machine. They ate and talked about their failure to find anything on the stairways yesterday or this morning.

Lured by the familiar opening sequence of a Bond movie, the three started watching the TV as they ate lunch. When the scene of James with his latest girl in a Murphy bed that folded against the wall played out, it gave the three men almost simultaneously a notion they hadn't even considered.

"Maybe one of the stairways folds giving access to the crawl space," Will said as his eyes lit up.

"That's got to be it," agreed Harv.

"What are we waiting for," Mike said as he chugged down the last of his can of soda.

Mike and Harv spent the rest of the day trying to lift the stairs in each floor. They had no success. Will wheeled just inside each of the doorways and looked on. Now on the top floor, he couldn't figure things out.

"There's got to be something we're missing," he said with a frustrated tone to his voice. "Why can't we find the access?"

"We'll have better luck tomorrow, maybe," said Mike. "I have some paperwork to do in the morning. I can't get away from the office until the afternoon."

Harv shook his head and raised his hands above his head, "Well, even if we find access, we are too big to crawl around in it."

"One step at a time, gentlemen," reminded Will. "Let's find how to get in first. Then we'll see what size person looks like they can fit in."

They headed for the elevators. The twins, Trudy, and Lucy were in the cab of the one that opened first.

"What's going on girls?" asked Mike.

"We're just going up and down," said Trudy.

"Yeah," added Lucy. "Up these and down those."

"Sounds like fun," laughed Harv.

"More fun than the stairways," added Trudy.

"But there are more places to hide in them," admitted Lucy.

"What do you mean?" asked Will.

Just then the elevator reached the lobby. "Bye," said the girls. They rushed out and got in another elevator.

Will raised his eyebrows and interjected a 'hmm.' "Looks like I need to add the twins to my list of people to talk with."

23

Mike had to spend some extra time in the office to make up for being gone during the past two days. Norma could handle mostly everything that came up, but some things required Mike's attention.

Harv invited Will to dine that evening with him and Suzanne. "We have the freezer full of frozen entrees," he said. "You can have your pick from any of them."

"Oh, TV dinners," laughed Will. "My favorite."

"See you about 6:30 then," Harv said. He headed for the mailroom.

"I'll be there," replied Will.

Will and Harv were reticent in talking with Suzanne at dinner. They only told her about the crawl space and the stairways. They said nothing about the diamonds.

"You ought to talk with Rose's twin girls," she said. "I see them on occasion going in and out of the stairs."

"Trudy and Lucy," said Will.

"Yes, they spend time with their grandmother Delores," added Suzanne. "Rose is her daughter. She's a nurse, you know."

Will rubbed the back of his neck when the idea popped into his head that the twins might be the key to finding access to the crawl space and breaking this case wide open. He asked Suzanne if she knew Delores well enough to ask her if it would be okay for him to talk with Trudy and Lucy.

"It might soften the blow if you already know her," suggested Will. "I've never met her."

Suzanne said she knew Delores a little bit from visiting with her in the laundry room, and that she would bring it up the next time she saw her.

A couple of days passed, and Suzanne never saw Delores. Finally, they crossed paths in the mailroom. When Suzanne told her who Will was, that he wanted to talk with the girls, and about the stairways, Delores got visibly shaken.

"I didn't see anything wrong with the girls keeping the earrings and the ring," she said. "They are just shiny, worthless jewelry they found."

"That wasn't what he wanted to talk to them about," Suzanne said. "It's something about them playing in the stairways."

"That's where they found the stuff," Delores admitted. "When they went exploring under the stairs."

That prompted Suzanne to say, "Let's have some coffee." She and Delores walked to the kitchen for a cup and a sit-down conversation.

Later when Suzanne went back up to the apartment, she informed Harv about the exchange she had with Delores. He immediately grabbed his phone to call Will.

"You need to come right up here," he told Will. "Suzanne talked with Delores. You won't believe what she found out."

Will was about to do his laundry, but now his dirty clothes could wait for another time. He put his basket back in the closet. He tossed his crossword puzzle book and pen on the counter. He always took them to the laundry room to help pass the time. Will went upstairs and barely made it in the door of the apartment before Harv eagerly offered him a beer.

"Come in, Suzanne has something to tell you," Harv quickly said.

She began by telling Will all about the earrings and the ring the girls had found. She then told him about the stairways.

"Isn't that something," Harv exclaimed. "Delores thinks the jewelry's not real."

Will hadn't intended for Suzanne to know about the jewelry. He was afraid word would spread too fast through the gossip and rumor mills. He now had to admit to her, since Harv brought it up, that the jewelry was real, but he didn't tell her of their value.

She put her hand over her mouth, "Oh, my, if they are real, then you better get them from the girls. They are probably worth a lot of money."

"Yes, you're right," Will said quickly before Harv could say anything else. "I bet they are."

Suzanne told Will that Delores was OK with him talking to the girls.

"Glad to hear that," Will said. He asked Suzanne to call Delores to find out when it was a good time to visit with them. Delores said she would talk to Rose about it and get back to her.

Rose agreed to talk to Will first. Curious to know the details before letting her girls talk with a retired detective in a wheelchair, she wanted to hear all the facts. Will saw her point. He gave it all to her straight. Rose decided it best to talk with her girls instead of letting Will.

"I think they'll be more honest and open with me," she said. "I imagine they'd be pretty defensive with you."

Will shook his head in agreement. She didn't say anything to the girls the next morning when she dropped them off at Grandma Delores' apartment.

She did bring pizza and ice cream, however, that late afternoon after her shift.

When supper ended Rose let the girls have TV time. They then had their baths and put on matching pajamas. Delores went into her room, shut the door, and began trying to read a book. She couldn't resist listening, though.

"Trudy, Lucy, tell me about finding those trinkets," Rose began as innocently as she could. "Where did you get them?"

The girls, sitting on the couch together, both squirmed. Trudy looked at the ceiling. Lucy turned ashen. They then looked at each other.

"Don't we get to keep them?" Trudy asked.

"Yeah," added Lucy. "We found them fair and square in the ..."

Trudy elbowed Lucy and she trailed off what she was about to say.

"In what?" asked Rose, still trying to be reserved. "You're not in trouble. I just want to know."

"In the secret passageway," confessed Lucy. "We found them in there."

"Secret passageway," echoed Rose. This time she leaned forward and had a bit more inquisitive tone to her voice. "What secret passageway?"

"Come on," Trudy said reaching out her hand to take Rose's. "We'll show you, and some other stuff, too."

"We didn't do anything wrong, honest," Lucy said almost whining.

"Of course not," Rose reassured her. She took her hand.

"Mom, we'll be back in a few minutes," Rose yelled to Delores. "The girls want to show me something."

And off they went. Delores wanted to come along but stayed behind. She started to call Suzanne. She put down the phone and went to her and Harv's apartment instead. She wanted to tell them what happened in person.

The girls took Rose to the stairwell on the west wing of their floor.

"We found one of these on every other set of stairs," Trudy said sort of sheepishly.

"But only on this side," added Lucy. "There aren't any on the other side." Both girls shook their heads.

"There's something else," Trudy said more eagerly now. "I'll show you."

"This is really cool," Lucy giggled.

Trudy pushed a button under the third step. The first three steps popped up about three feet. Lucy then pulled a lever on the fourth step. It caused the remainder of the stairs to bump up a few inches. The girls together pushed them up, and the steps rose enough to reveal a three-foot circular hole in the wall.

"See, it's a secret passageway with steps to climb up and down all the way," revealed Lucy. "Once you get up there you can even crawl across the top."

"It's scary, but fun," said Trudy. "You come down the other side. Go down to the lobby. We'll show you."

"Whoa, whoa, slow down," said Rose. "What about the earrings and the ring?"

"We'll show you," repeated Trudy. "Go down to the lobby."

Lucy had already gone into the crawlspace. Trudy followed. Rose, a bit bewildered, walked to the elevators. On her way down she called Delores.

"Mom, come down to the lobby right now," Rose almost yelled. "Hurry."

"What for?" Delores asked anxiously. "Goodness, you sound alarmed. Is something wrong?"

"No, no, just what the girls have shown me," answered Rose. "You won't believe it. Hurry up."

Suzanne and Harv overheard what Delores said. "What's wrong?" asked Suzanne.

"Is there something the matter?" Harv added.

"I don't know, but I'm supposed to go down to the lobby," said Delores. "Something about the girls."

"We're going with you," Suzanne said as she looked at Harv.

He nodded with agreement. They walked to the elevators. The one that opened first was full of three ladies and their rollators that Harv recognized.

He felt comfortable saying, "You all headed outside for a smoke?"

The doors closed before they could answer, but he saw them all smile. The next elevator seemed to take forever to reach them, but they got down to the lobby before the girls emerged from their journey.

24

Malcolm, on duty filling in second shift for Paul who had the flu, became curious about the gathering.

"Gie's yer patter?" he said with a heavy Scottish brogue.

They all looked at him. Harv quizzically said, "Huh?"

"What's going on?" Malcolm replied without his accent.

Suddenly they heard knocking. It seemed to be coming from the wall where a mirror hung between the restrooms. A few seconds later Trudy came out of the woman's restroom with a box containing pills and shouted, "Ta Da!"

"Come out, come out, wherever you are," she then chanted.

Lucy came out of the men's restroom skipping and singing, *"Skidamarinky dinky dink, skidamarinky doo!"*

Delores ran into the men's restroom to see what was going on. She got an eyeful. There was a doorway open in the wall in the handicapped stall that led to a tiny room. Another open doorway on the other side went into the women's restroom. A rope ladder hung from an opening in the ceiling. She didn't notice the two-way mirror at first glance because she picked up another box containing pills.

"Get Will down here PDQ," she hollered. "He's got to see this."

Delores met Will at the elevator. She gave him the boxes. She then told him the whole story and showed him the tiny room between the restrooms. The first thing he thought of when he heard it all and saw the room was Hazel and her "rats.' Then the pieces started to fit together.

"Herb," he thought to himself. Will figured the pills must be an opioid but was going to have the lab downtown test them to be sure. He turned his wheelchair and went to the security desk.

"Malcolm," Will said confidently, "I think I have it figured out."

"Aye," replied Malcolm, "The wee barras, a nod's as guid as a wink tae a blind horse."

"If you said the children don't know what is going on, then I agree with you," Will nodded.

"Aye, that's close enough." Malcolm then stood up and politely told everyone to go back to their apartments.

Delores looked at Will and said, "Are those what I think they are?"

He nodded his head and said to her, "Thank goodness the twins didn't get into them. I think they're opioids from Herb, Ethel's late husband."

The girls ran to the elevators first to push the buttons. When they both opened Trudy said to Lucy, "Let's race."

The girls left their grandma, mother, and everyone else waiting. It took a couple of minutes for the elevators to go all the way up. Only one of them, however, came back down. When it opened both girls screamed, "Surprise!"

"I think we've had enough excitement for one night," Rose said as they all piled in one elevator.

"Well," said Malcolm without a trace of Scottish accent, "Tell me all about it."

"I need to look over my notes and get it all together first," Will said. "It's all on my computer, napkins, and note pads."

"I'm going on vacation," Malcolm said. "I suppose it will have to wait until I get back."

Margie, who just moved in the week before, came in the front doors. She had been at her sister's house all day. Margie had a raspy voice from smoking all her life. Her clothes smelled of cigarette smoke. She even unconsciously held the first two fingers of her left hand apart when she wasn't smoking, which was rare considering she smoked two packs a day. She tried to hide her smell by wearing too much perfume.

"I'm going to make some hot tea, and then off to bed," she said. "Malcolm, what are you doing here? It's not midnight yet."

"I'm working second shift today," he said. "I have an early flight to catch in the morning. I'm going on vacation."

"Oh," said Margie. "Where are you going and how long are you going to be gone?"

"Uh," Malcolm hesitated. "I'm not going to tell. You might follow me." He then laughed.

Will waited for Margie to go into the kitchen. "Let's take a closer look in the restrooms," he then said to Malcolm. "I want you to see before I go back up."

"Crivens," Malcolm exclaimed in astonishment, "A two-way mirror and a climbing hatch in the ceiling."

"It's always been there and the crawlspace, too," Will said. "Amazing that it has gone undetected all this time."

"Amazing," echoed Malcolm.

"Yeah, amazing," Will came back with. He had a serious tone to his voice.

"Well, somebody knew about it," Malcolm concluded. "All the crazy stories from the residents make sense now."

"Yeah, somebody," Will said just as seriously as he had just expressed himself.

Malcom thought for a moment. "Maybe you need to talk with the maintenance staff. They have access to all the rooms. Nobody gives a second thought to them being in everybody's place."

Will noticed that a bead of sweat had run down the left side of Malcolm's face.

"Yeah, maybe," Will said looking straight into Malcolm's eyes.

Will went back up to his apartment. He placed the boxes of pills with the jewelry. He spent most of the night going through all his notes to help him recall what the residents he had talked with had said. He gave much thought to Malcolm and why he seemed a bit out of sorts. The back of his neck gave him an indication to pursue it further.

Will wrote a point-by-point outline to make clear to him not only what he thought happened to Ethel, but also a plausible how and why. He wanted to be as careful, concise, and complete as possible when he explained it to Mike and Norma.

25

Will went down to the office the next morning as soon as it opened. He asked Norma to bring cups of coffee for them all. When she returned, tray in hand, he told her to shut the door.

"Norma, your suspicions were right," he began. "I don't think Ethel's death was an accident by her own hand."

"So, it <u>was</u> murder after all," she said.

"Ethel wasn't killed for her diamonds, though," Will said. "But by a robber mainly after something more expensive."

"What do you mean?" Norma asked.

"I figure Ethel was taking an afternoon nap. The robber crawled up to her room and went in through the secret doorway in the back of the closet."

"Wait a minute," Mike stopped Will. "What secret doorway?"

"The one that is in each end apartment on the west wing, including yours," Will added.

"What?" Mike exclaimed.

"I'll show you everything, just wait," Will fired back.

"The robber was really after these pills," Will deduced. "Herb confiscated pills from the drug bust back in '77 but didn't turn them in. He then got into the illegal pill business by the lure of all the money."

"How do you know this for sure?" asked Norma.

"All the stories I heard from all these wacky residents started to fit together," said Will. "The topper was the twins."

"What?" Mike exclaimed again.

"She went into Ethel's apartment to get the pills she was passing around for a price," Will said.

"She?" Mike asked perplexed.

Will put up his hand and interrupted Mike. "Yes, she."

"She who? Norma asked.

"When I finish, you'll be able to guess who," Will said relishing the moment. "She couldn't find any pills, so she took the diamonds instead."

Will continued, "Here's where it didn't go quite right, I think. The robber lit a match, threw it where Ethel was sleeping, and quickly closed the secret doorway. But the explosion caused her to lose her balance and drop the diamonds. They fell all the way down to the ground."

Will then told in detail about the cats and Sadie. Mike and Norma could hardly believe it.

"You've got to be kidding," Norma said while shaking her head. "This is just too much."

"I'm not finished," Will said.

He told about Bill's and Glady's time in New York, the robberies there, and them not showing up in Florida.

"Oh my gosh," Norma, said, "The she is Gladys?"

"But where are they?" Norma added.

"I don't know … yet!" said Will. "But I intend to find out."

"Bill and Gladys in cahoots to rob and kill poor Ethel," Norma looked at Mike. "I just can't imagine."

"How do you know it was Gladys, and not Bill?" asked Mike. "Or Billy Bud."

"Yeah, the bed bug guy is kind of creepy," Norma said. "I go with him when he inspects, and he gives me the chills."

"Funny you should mention Billy Bud," Will chuckled. "He was in on it, too."

"How?" asked Mike.

"He was distributing pills," Will said. "Think about it. He was in and out of every apartment."

"Gladys is small and athletic enough to have fit in and roam around the crawlspace?" Norma questioned. "Billy Bud is skinny, but I don't see him committing murder."

"Exactly," answered Will. "You hit the nail on the head. The pieces all fit together."

"Gladys committed the robberies at the hotel in New York," Norma surmised. "I get it now."

Will took Mike and Norma outside to see the hole the cats had dug. He then took them to the stairways and showed how the girls found access to the crawlspace. He then gathered them in Mike's apartment and revealed the doorway in the closet.

"All of these end apartments have been updated a couple of times since the building opened," Norma brought up. "Wouldn't somebody working have seen this?"

"I talked with Lopez. He said the only thing they do to the bedroom closets is paint them and put up these metal rods," Will answered. "You have to push hard to open the back wall, harder than just stroking a paint brush or roller."

Mike pushed hard and, sure enough, the wall opened and there was, indeed, a crawlspace.

"Oh my gosh," he said. "Look at that, wow."

When they all made it back to the lobby Will told them he had one more surprise.

"Don't go in your offices yet," he said and excused himself to the men's room.

Mike and Norma looked at each other wondering why they had to stay in the lobby. They soon found out. Will went in the men's door but came out the women's door.

"How?"

"What in the world?"

"Come on in," he said. "There's a tiny room in between the two restrooms."

Mike and Norma took turns going in and looking around. The space was too small for them to go in together. They were amazed. And then Will pointed at the two-way mirror. They were even more amazed.

"Agnes always said that's a two-way mirror," Norma laughed. "The old coot isn't so crazy, after all."

"This explains all the stories about voices and footsteps," Mike said.

"And rats, too," Norma added.

"Let's keep this amongst ourselves for now," Will alerted. "Nobody needs to know yet."

"Absolutely," Mike said. Norma agreed.

"And to think I was going to leave this place," said Norma. "No way, not now."

"Well, there's more, too," Will said to Norma and Mike. But since it was office time residents were milling about and the phones were ringing. Norma and Mike had to go back to work, and it was business as usual, sort of.

"I'll tell you the rest later," Will said to them with a smile on his face and feeling a bit full of himself.

He went up to his apartment. He called downtown to the police department and talked to a former detective friend of his. He told her the whole story and asked her to get flight information on Malcolm and then to book him on the next flight to the same destination. He then went up to visit the twins. Rose had told him that they had drawn and colored pictures of the feral cats to give him.

"This is Mumu and Spots," said Trudy. "And this one is Soda Pop," said Lucy.

Will thanked the girls and invited them with Rose's permission to his apartment to put the pictures on his refrigerator door. Will had four finished jigsaw puzzles of cats glued and pinned on his kitchen walls.

The girls saw them, and Trudy said, "Hey, maybe we should make our pictures into jigsaw puzzles."

Epilogue

Bill and Gladys sat at an outdoor table at the restaurant in the Checon quarter of Nuevo Gerona. The Caribbean Sea in the distance looked bright blue and blended in on the horizon to match the color of the sky. A soft breeze seemed to caress them as they drank their Mojitos. This island off the west coast of Cuba seemed so peaceful and pleasant to them.

"I'm looking forward to having the grilled alligator today," said Bill as he raised his glass and clinked it against Gladys'. "I think you should put the mint garnish from our drinks in your hair."

Being coy, Gladys smiled, winked her eye, and said, "Don't you think this blond wig is enough?"

"Well," laughed Bill. "I suppose you're right." He rubbed his black goatee and flicked his eyebrows. His widow's peak was gone. He had dyed his hair, grown it longer, and combed it to the side.

"Quit being silly," Gladys said being persnickety. "It's only lunchtime."

The waiter served Gladys her jambalaya. "Authentic creole style senorita," he said.

He then placed a plate of cut up grilled alligator for Bill, "very lean today, senor."

"Muy bueno," said Bill.

"Bien, gracias," said Gladys.

"What shall we do this afternoon?" Bill asked Gladys.

"I don't know," Gladys shrugged her shoulders. "Why don't we wait for the grandkids and let them decide."

A few minutes later Malcolm arrived sans red wig and Scottish accent.

"Well," Bill said. "Shall we go to the museum or a baseball game?

"I think Billy Bud will want to go to the ball game," Malcolm said.

Appendix

"Our Three Dads"

"When I was a kid, I walked half a mile to get a block of coal for the stove to heat the upstairs room where we lived.

Your older brother, when he was my age, carried coal only three blocks in the basket of his bike for the basement furnace to heat the small house where they lived.

You only had to hit a switch in the hallway to turn on the heat in the big house where you lived."

> ~ *The oldest brother Fred talking to the youngest brother Joey at their dad's funeral.*

Dad, the third of five boys all born from 1904 to 1910, began losing his hair first. Although they all would eventually end up bald, Harold "wore a hat" before any of them.

After childhoods of swimming in the river, playing stickball, climbing trees, causing as much trouble at school as possible, and visiting their police Sergeant dad as he walked his beat on the deepest part of the downtown, the boys formed a bond that would last forever. The fact all of them shared a room during those times had something to do with that as well.

As the years passed childhood activities gave way to smoking, drinking, and wearing Oxford suits with black and white shoes called "gangsters." Straw hats morphed into fedoras and the Walker boys had as good a time as anyone of any age during the late 1920s in the middle of Prohibition. They certainly looked the part.

On a loud night at a speakeasy south of the city that let just about everyone in who looked the part, the boys tried to out smoke and out drink each other to look more grown up. Harold, between puffs of unfiltered cigarettes and sips of bourbon, saw a black-haired girl dancing the Charleston with a group of girls. She had an air about her that the other girls did not. Plus, her pink dress and matching cloche hat drew attention to her.

He approached her all decked out with his fedora, wide white tie, pinstripe suit, and black and white shoes. He grabbed her right hand and began twirling her around. The other girls giggled, gave them room, and clapped to the music hollering *"Margie, Margie."* She smiled and they danced to the added cheers of *"Harold, Harold"* from his three brothers at the table across the room and down a step from the dance floor.

The group of girls, Margie's four older sisters, sensing that the evening would go on without the company of their youngest sis, scurried back to their table, up a step and away from the dance floor. They continued giggling and talking amongst themselves as they sipped their soda pops.

"That's quite a group of your friends," Harold said while they danced.

"Oh, those are all my sisters," Margie answered. *"We're the Bromley girls."*

They laughed and Harold added, *"Well, well, those are my brothers at the table and we're the Walker boys."*

Thus began a relationship that would last a lifetime. Harold and Margie passed, with flying colors, the early parts of their time together. It blossomed in only a month to the meet-the-parents stage. Harold's parents, not amused upon meeting Margie, did not approve of him dating a Catholic girl who attended a parochial school on the east side of the city.

His dad made it quite clear about, *"those kind of people"* to Harold when he returned that night after taking Margie home.

Mom reinforced the feeling with, *"Why can't you find a nice girl at your school."*

Likewise, Margie's parents did not approve of her dating a boy from the inner-city public school that had a reputation, as her dad said, for *"drop-outs and hoodlums."*

Her mom also showed dismay with, *"Why can't you find a nice boy at your school."*

This mutual parental disapproval made the young couple even more determined to stay together, so together that Margie got pregnant in April of 1931 just two months before high school graduation. When Harold got the news a month later from Margie, he panicked and dropped out. With only a month to go to his graduation he headed out of town, out of state, and hopefully, out of touch.

The bus he rode zig zagged several highways through Illinois and then across Hwy 40 through Missouri. Out of money at Kansas City, Harold got off the bus for good. Stranded and broke, he spent four nights at a Salvation Army shelter just down the street from the depot. A Lieutenant there found him a job on the fifth day working on the rails of the Hannibal Bridge.

Meanwhile back home, his brothers along with the city police spent the first two days hitting all the local areas where Harold might be. The boys deep down, though, suspected that he probably had bolted out of town. Harold's dad then contacted area police as well as the state police, and the search widened. The rest of the week passed with nobody having any leads.

The two families decided to have a meeting together. One of the Walker brothers started it with, *"I bet he headed west."*

Another brother followed up with, *"probably took a bus."*

Margie added, *"but he didn't have much money."*

Her dad, exasperated, barked, *"Then Sergeant Walker why don't you check the bus depot for buses going west."*

"Maybe he hopped a train," Margie blurted. *"Or he could have just hitchhiked."*

She began to cry. Silence ensued for a couple of seconds and then Margie's mom said, *"We'll find him, honey, and then ...,"* she stopped herself short of saying anymore.

Finally, after a couple more days, reports began to come in. Harold was seen at the bus depot in Mt. Vernon, Illinois; St. Louis; Springfield, Missouri; and Kansas City but not further west in Topeka or Salina. This prompted Harold's dad to contact the police in Kansas City and neighboring Independence, Missouri.

The next day he got word from the Kansas City Police Department that Salvation Army personnel interviewed reported that Harold had stayed at one of their shelters four nights and that they got him a job working for the railroad.

Harold's dad, in full uniform, and Margie's dad got into his Studebaker Roadster that afternoon and drove straight through the night and next morning headed for Kansas City. They talked back and forth about what to do once they found Harold. During a stop in Rolla, Missouri, for breakfast they decided to bring Harold back, have him marry Margie, and live with her parents.

"We have an attic above our grocery store," Mr. Bromley stated. *"They can take turns working for us and caring for the baby upstairs."*

"I'll pay for all the baby's needs and then some," said Sergeant Walker.

The two men reluctantly agreed, but discussion about their differences of religion, politics, and lifestyle filled much of the time all the way to KC.

They agreed on one other thing. Go to the Kansas City Police Department and for more dramatic effect have their officers find Harold and bring him in under the guise that he would be in a lineup. It didn't take long for the KCPD with the cooperation of the railroad authorities to do just that.

Harold looked shocked when he saw his dad and Margie's dad at the police station.

"Oh no, I'm not going back with you two," he shouted.

"Oh, yes you are," fired back his dad.

"And you're going to marry my daughter," Mr. Bromley chimed in.

Sergeant Walker called home to tell his wife that they had found Harold. She passed on the news to Margie's mom. The Walker boys and the Bromley girls got the word, too.

The homecoming went well. Harold agreed to marry Margie. The car ride from KC with all alternatives outlined in detail by the two dads convinced him. Margie had talked with her mom and sisters, too, and they came to the same conclusion after all the scenarios got banted about.

Harold's parents had no intention of their son turning Catholic. Likewise, the Walker's would not agree to a Protestant wedding. After much heated discussion they all agreed on a Justice of the Peace wedding. While this didn't sit well with Margie's parents and sisters, she convinced them that it would work out.

"*Don't worry,*" she said slyly, "*I will get Harold to see things my way.*"

A June wedding in the courthouse happened with two sets of dismayed looking parents, four sisters faking happiness, and three brothers feeling proud attending as witnesses. A two-day honeymoon occurred with a drive south across the newly constructed bridge over the Ohio River to a Kentucky mom and pop motel.

The young couple settled in the scantily furnished attic of the grocery store. Summer then Fall passed. Winter began and in January of 1932 Frederick Robert was born.

Printed in the USA
CPSIA information can be obtained
at www.ICGtesting.com
LVHW020324011123
762706LV00010B/60